"Regardless of what your reasons were for signing the contract, you did so. And while you were only eighteen, you were not a minor. You are obligated to its terms unless both parties agree to different ones."

"I will not marry either of your brothers."

"I am glad you did not include me in that categorical refusal." His smile was more like an apex predator baring its teeth.

"You?" Nataliya asked faintly.

No, Nikolai could not be saying what Nataliya thought he was saying. "You're not a prince." The contract stipulated a prince. "You're a king." Her voice rose and cracked on the word *king*, but seriously...?

He had to be joking.

Princesses by Royal Decree

Their place at the royal altar awaits...

The time has come for royal brothers King Nikolai and Princes Konstantin and Dimitri of Mirrus to wed. Their journeys to the altar will be just as they rule—by royal decree!

Lady Nataliya was contracted to marry a prince from Mirrus but is shocked when King Nikolai, whom she's secretly desired for years, steps in instead!

Emma's affair with Prince Konstantin is forced to end when his duty calls, but she's carrying a secret that will bind them forever!

Jenna's a fashion journalist and has no desire to be a princess, but her interest in Prince Dimitri could change everything...

Read Nataliya and Nikolai's story in
Queen by Royal Appointment
Available now!

Look out for Emma's and Jenna's stories, coming soon!

And you can revisit Nataliya's royal family of Volyarus in Lucy Monroe's previous titles
One Night Heir and *Prince of Secrets*.

Lucy Monroe

QUEEN BY ROYAL APPOINTMENT

HARLEQUIN®
PRESENTS®

Recycling programs
for this product may
not exist in your area.

ISBN-13: 978-1-335-40421-3

Queen by Royal Appointment

Copyright © 2021 by Lucy Monroe

This edition published by arrangement with Harlequin Books S.A.

For questions and comments about the quality of this book,
please contact us at CustomerService@Harlequin.com.

Harlequin Enterprises ULC
22 Adelaide St. West, 40th Floor
Toronto, Ontario M5H 4E3, Canada
www.Harlequin.com

Printed in U.S.A.

USA TODAY bestselling author **Lucy Monroe** lives and writes in the gorgeous Pacific Northwest. While she loves her home, she delights in experiencing different cultures and places in her travels, which she happily shares with her readers through her books. A lifelong devotee of the romance genre, Lucy can't imagine a more fulfilling career than writing the stories in her head for her readers to enjoy.

Books by Lucy Monroe

Harlequin Presents

Million Dollar Christmas Proposal
Kosta's Convenient Bride
The Spaniard's Pleasurable Vengeance
After the Billionaire's Wedding Vows...

Ruthless Russians

An Heiress for His Empire
A Virgin for His Prize

Visit the Author Profile page
at Harlequin.com for more titles.

For my bestie and the sister of my heart, Carolyn.
I'm just so grateful to have you in my life.
Much love!

CHAPTER ONE

LADY NATALIYA SHEVCHENKO stood outside the private reception room in the Volyarus palace, feeling more like she was entering a war tribunal than going to the family meeting her "uncle," King Fedir, had decreed she attend.

And she was the one about to be on trial for Acts Against the State.

Only, legally, she'd done nothing wrong. Morally, she hadn't either, but she did not expect "Uncle" Fedir to agree.

King Fedir wasn't actually her uncle. He was her mother's cousin, but the two had been raised as close as siblings and he had always called himself Nataliya's uncle.

Taking a deep breath and centering herself, calling on a lifetime of training and all her courage, she indicated with a nod of her head for the guard to pull the ornate door open. His very presence indicated that there were more people in that room than her family.

Unless palace security had changed drastically, family only meant guards at either end of the hall, which there were, so this one meant more dignitaries inside.

Two guesses for who those dignitaries were and she would only need one.

Head held high, Nataliya walked into the luxuriously appointed room. No one would mistake this space with its silk wallpaper, and gilt and brocade furniture, for anything other than a royal's.

Her heels clicked against the marble, before stepping onto the lush carpet that filled the center of the room.

King Fedir sat in an ornate armchair that might as well have been his throne, for all his regal bearing. Except that glower he was giving her. That didn't look so much regal as just really, really annoyed. To his right sat Queen Oxana, her expression entirely enigmatic.

Nataliya's own mother was there too. First cousin to the King and Oxana's best friend, Solomia, Countess Shevchenko, nevertheless occupied a seat of no distinction.

Further from the royal couple than the youngest son of Prince Evengi of Mirrus, the other major player in this farce of judgment, Nataliya's mother sat in an armchair away from everyone else. Whether that had been by her choice or the King's, Nataliya would figure out later.

Right now, she surveyed the other occupants of the opulent room. Prince Evengi, former King of Mirrus, and his three sons sat opposite King Fedir and Queen Oxana. Although Prince Evengi had abdicated his throne to his eldest son, Nikolai, nearly a decade ago, there was no doubt that he was the driving force behind the contract Nataliya and her parents had signed.

A contract that stipulated, among other business and

private concerns, that Nataliya would wed the second son to the House of Merikov, Konstantın.

Rumored to be descendants of both Romanov and Deminov blood, the Russian family had established their kingdom on an island between Alaska and Russia, like Volyarus, but Mirrus was in the Chukchi Sea.

They had another thing in common with Volyarus. The basis of their economy had started with mining rare minerals and was now just as profitable a worldwide concern, if not quite as stable as Yurkovich-Tanner, the company that supported Volyarus' economy.

Despite the Ukrainian heritage of Volyarus and its not so amicable history with Russia, King Fedir was determined to cement a family and business alliance with Mirrus, even ten years after that draconian contract was signed.

The only other two occupants of the room were her "uncle's" sons, Maksim, Crown Prince, and his elder brother, the adopted Prince Demyan.

There was a time that their families had been very close.

Although, Nataliya worked for Demyan and saw Maks and his wife on occasion when they were in Seattle, that closeness had been gone for many years.

Breaking protocol, Nataliya ignored the assembled Kings present and smiled her first greeting to her mother. "Hello, Mama. You look well."

"Thank you, Nataliya. It is always good to see you." Mama smiled back, but the expression did not reach her worried eyes, the same warm brown as Nataliya's.

Nataliya was not surprised her father had not been summoned. He was, for all intents and purposes, a nonentity in her life and still very much a persona non grata in Volyarus.

Fifteen years ago, his decision to abandon his Countess and their child to pursue marriage to his most recent mistress had broken the cardinal rules of discretion and putting duty to country above personal considerations.

He had brought ugly attention to the royal family and the throne, and for that, Nataliya doubted he would ever be forgiven.

After greeting her mother, Nataliya gave King Fedir and Queen Oxana her full regard, dropping into a perfect curtsy between their two chairs. "Uncle Fedir, Aunt Oxana, it is a pleasure to see you again."

That might be stretching the truth a bit. And under the circumstance, she had no doubt the man who was in actuality her first cousin, once removed was regretting not rescinding the courtesy title of uncle long before now.

"Nataliya…" King Fedir actually looked at a loss for words, for the first time in Nataliya's memory. He certainly hadn't been the last time they'd spoken.

That time during a phone call, she'd had to schedule two weeks in advance.

She might call him *uncle*, but she didn't enjoy family privileges any longer.

When the silence had stretched, Queen Oxana gave an unreadable look to her husband and stood.

In a move that shocked Nataliya, the Queen approached her in order to give Nataliya the traditional kiss of greeting on both cheeks. "My dear, it is good to see you." The Queen's voice held no insincerity. "Come, you will sit beside me."

The Queen gave a look to her son Maksim, indicating with a regal inclination of her head a couple of equally elegant flicks of her wrist what she wanted done. Despite being Crown Prince, Maks immediately jumped up and oversaw the moving of chairs so that Nataliya's mother sat on her other side, thus cementing in the minds of everyone present just where the Queen stood on the issue to be discussed.

Nataliya's scandalous behavior that had not in fact been scandalous at all.

The King did not look pleased by this turn of events, but Nataliya did not care.

His lack of true concern for her and her mother had been shown fifteen years ago, when they had been forced to emigrate to the States to *protect the good name of the royal family*. Though neither were responsible for the gutter press dragging their names through the mud.

No one spoke for several interminable minutes while both of the older Kings looked on at Nataliya in censure. King Nikolai had a better poker face than even Oxana, however.

Nataliya had no idea what the current King of Mirrus thought of the proceedings and what had prompted them, but even his unreadable regard did things to Nataliya's insides she wished, for the hundredth time at least, it did not.

And because she never lied to herself, she did not try to believe she did not care what that was. He was not the man she was supposed to marry, but he was the only man in the House of Merikov whose opinion carried any weight with her.

When she did not let the clearly strategic silence force her into speech, King Fedir frowned. "You know why you are here?"

"I prefer not to guess."

"You signed a contract promising marriage to Prince Konstantin."

"I did." Though if any man did not live up to his name, it was the one she was not engaged to, but still expected to marry one day. "Ten years ago," she added, letting her tone tell them all what she thought of a decade-long wait for that contract to be fulfilled and yet her being here because she'd done what? Gone on a few dates?

Not that she hadn't wanted just this reaction, but seriously?

Get real.

A very unroyal-like sound came from Prince Evengi. "Then explain yourself."

Nataliya stood and gave the King a curtsy, acknowledging him formally, before returning to her seat. One must observe the niceties. "What would you like me to explain?" she asked.

"Do not play obtuse," he barked.

King Nikolai said something in an undertone to his father and the older man yanked his head in acknowledgement.

Prince Konstantin, current heir to his brother's throne, frowned at Nataliya. "You know very well why you have been summoned here, why we have all had to take time from our busy schedules to deal with this mess."

"What mess might that be?" she asked, unimpressed.

Had she curtsied to him? No, she had not and the ice cap on Mount Volyarus would melt before she did.

This man lived and breathed the company that made up the majority of his country's economy. The time he'd taken for his affairs had been negligible and Nataliya had felt no actual envy toward the women he'd taken to his bed and done nothing else to romance.

Ten years ago, she had signed that draconian contract for two equally important reasons. Ten years in which this man had not even made enough time in his schedule to announce the engagement. Ten years during which Nataliya had lived in a stasis that had not upset her all that much, honestly.

Her mother's limbo, she was not so sanguine about. Because one of the clauses of the contract was that Countess Solomia would be able to return to Volyarus upon the marriage of her daughter to the Prince of the House of Merikov.

Without the formalized engagement, much less a marriage, that had not happened.

Her second reason had been no less successful. Nataliya had hoped that by agreeing to marry Konstantin, her inappropriate feelings for his married brother would go away.

While she'd gotten over Nikolai, it wasn't because of her commitment to Konstantin.

"This mess." Konstantin threw down the fashion magazine that had run the "50 First Dates for a Would-Be Princess" article.

"Are you hoping to claim that in the past ten years, you have not dated anyone, Prince Konstantin?" she asked him, with little interest in his answer and aware that the term *date* was in fact a misnomer. "Only I have a whole file full of pictures that would indicate otherwise."

"You had me followed?" he asked with fury, surging to his feet.

Only his brother's hand on his arm kept the angry Prince across the room.

She should probably be intimidated, but anger and posturing held no sway with a woman who had endured years in her father's household. She could have told her erstwhile intended that.

His position as Prince was no more impressive to Nataliya. She'd been raised as part of the royal family of Volyarus until the age of thirteen and had never ceased being the daughter of nobility.

"Perhaps you would like to explain, Uncle Fedir?" she prompted, her own anger a wall of cold ice around her heart, making her voice arctic.

And she did not regret that. At all.

The King of Volyarus winced as his own family and that of the other royal family present gave him varying looks of anger and condemnation.

"Of course we kept track of Prince Konstantin, but it was in no way nefarious." He made a dismissive gesture. "I have no doubt you had your interests watched, as well." He indicated Nataliya with a tip of his head.

She wasn't offended being referred to in that manner. The King's ability to hurt her had passed years ago.

"You shared your investigator's findings with your niece?" Nikolai asked, his voice laced with censure, but no shock at the other royal's actions.

If he'd given a bit of that censure to his brother, Nataliya would have respected him more. And something in her expression must have told him so because he gave her a strange look.

"I did not," King Fedir denied categorically.

"Then how?"

"I believe I can answer that," Prince Demyan, who had remained silent up until then, said.

Interesting that her mother and Queen Oxana were the only other women who had been invited to this ludicrous tribunal.

King Fedir stared at his other son. "How?" he barked.

"You know I use hackers to watch over our interests," Prince Demyan said, clearly unafraid of making such an admission in the rarified company.

Not one of these royals would voluntarily share *anything* being said in this room right now.

King Fedir nodded with a single jerk of his head.

"Nataliya is one of those hackers."

"The best one," Nataliya added. "Not to put too fine a point on it."

Demyan actually smiled at her, but then they were still friends, if no longer as close as siblings. "Yes, the best one."

"You did not assign her to watch over her own errant fiancé," the King asked, obviously appalled at the idea.

"He is *not* my fiancé," Nataliya said fiercely.

"No!" Demyan said at the same time.

"Then how?" Her uncle looked at her. He had asked her the first time she'd brought the photos to his attention.

She'd avoided answering then, not wanting a lecture about her actions to derail the reason for their discussion. She'd still hoped he would put her happiness somewhere in the realm of his priorities three months ago. Now she had no such illusions.

She shrugged. "I like to practice my skills. I was looking through files and noticed one with his name on it."

Everyone in the room seemed shocked by her actions.

"You hacked into your King's private files?" Nikolai asked, nothing in his tone indicating what he thought about that.

But his deep voice reverberated through her being nonetheless. If she could have chosen one person *not* to be here for this farce, it would be King Nikolai of Mirrus.

"Not exactly. I hacked into Demyan's files." She frowned. "In fact, I was looking for security breach points. To shore them up. I *like* Demyan. I did not want him to be vulnerable to other corporate or politically motivated hackers."

"Thank you," Demyan said amidst gasps and condemnation by others.

"And so because you were angry my son had not paid you enough attention since signing the contract, and in a misguided fit of jealousy and feminine pique, you thought to embarrass him into action?"

She stared at the old King of Mirrus, flabbergasted at his interpretation of her actions.

"You think I was *jealous*?" she asked in icy disbelief she made no effort to soften.

"Naturally," Konstantin said, ignoring her tone as he had her person for the past decade. "Only you miscalculated my reaction."

"Did I?" she asked, doubting very much that she had.

"Your weekly online auction of the items I sent to you in my effort to court you prior to announcing our formal engagement made me look the fool."

The *wooing* gifts had started arriving exactly one month after her appeal to King Fedir to renegotiate the terms of the contract, no doubt prompted by him. Konstantin's attempt at courtship had been as impersonal as the greeting between strangers at a State function and with even less effort put behind it.

"The proceeds go to a very deserving charity," she pointed out, not at all unhappy with the direction this conversation was heading, and not particularly bothered that Konstantin had found her disposal of the gifts inappropriate.

Maksim swore, a pithy Ukrainian curse that shocked the people around him. But he was looking at Nataliya with reluctant respect. He knew.

Nataliya couldn't help smiling at the man who had been as close as a brother until she was thirteen years old, and her entire family was ripped from her. She even winked.

He laughed.

"You find this amusing?" Prince Konstantin asked with angry reproach.

"I find this situation laughable, yes," Maksim said without apology in his manner, or tone.

And Nataliya wondered if the future King of Volyarus was more reasonable than his father and understood how over-the-top everyone's reaction was.

Not that she had not relied on that extreme reaction, but she still found it archaic, chauvinistic and not just a little ridiculous. Her manipulations would not have been possible if a gross double standard did not exist in the minds of almost every male in this room.

"You think your cousin is amusing, though her actions have destroyed our families' plans of a merger?" Konstantin asked furiously.

"Oh, there will be a business merger," Demyan said before his brother could answer. "Both our countries will benefit, but more to the point, Mirrus cannot afford to back out. The repercussions would be devastating for Mirrus Global and your country's economy."

"I will not marry her," Konstantin said implacably.

His father looked pained, and his brother, the King, frowned, but Nataliya felt elation pour through her. She had won. Because regardless of what the rest of the people in this room wanted, his words had just released *her* from her promise. And ultimately, that was all that mattered to her.

She'd only been eighteen, but she'd signed the contract in good faith and had been unwilling to simply renege. Her integrity would not allow it. She was not her father.

King Fedir suddenly looked old, and tired in a way she'd never noticed before. "That is exactly what you wanted, though, wasn't it?" he asked her.

"I could have done without the name calling and disgusting double standard, but yes."

King Fedir shook his head, clearly confused by her reaction. "I thought you wanted your mother settled back in her home country."

"Ten years ago, I wanted that more than anything. *I* wanted to come home, or at least be able to visit often."

"And that has changed?" King Fedir asked, sounding as fatigued as he looked.

"My mother has finally found peace with her life in America."

Queen Oxana looked wounded. "You don't want to come home?" she asked her best friend of more than thirty years.

Mama drew herself up, her dignity settled around her like a force field, making Nataliya nothing but proud. "My home is in America now."

"You do not mean that." Queen Oxana had the effrontery to sound hurt when she'd done nothing to stop Mama and Nataliya's exile fifteen years ago.

"I do."

"She does," Nataliya said with satisfaction, and was so happy about that she could cry. "You and your husband exiled my mother and me for the sins of my father. And though he knew how important that clause in the contract was to us both, he made no effort to press for fulfillment of the marriage merger." Now it would not happen at all.

Queen Oxana's expression was troubled. "You were too young to tie down to marriage when it was signed."

"But not too young to sign it? Not too young to be used as a political and business pawn?" Nataliya shook her head in disbelief.

"We all have duty we must adhere to," the Queen said, though with less fervent conviction than she used to.

"Our duty included exile. Looking back, I realize that asking more of my daughter was obscene." Mama could do regal disapproval as well as any queen.

"You know why we had to ask the sacrifice of you," King Fedir said to his cousin.

But Mama made Nataliya so proud yet again when she shook her head. "No, I never understood your decision to sacrifice me, a woman who was a better sister to you than Svitlana ever was. I spent years grieving the loss of my homeland, but I grieve no longer."

"And so you decided to break the contract?" Nikolai asked, this time his opinion clear for any to hear the disapproval and disappointment in his tone.

Nataliya met his gaze squarely. "My mother told me five years ago that she was not sure she would move back to Volyarus permanently, even if she could."

His brows drew together in a thoughtful frown. "Then what prompted your dating and the very public rejection of my brother's attempt to court you?"

"There is so much wrong with that question, I don't even know where to start." Was he as draconian as his father?

Nataliya had never believed it of Nikolai.

"Try. Please."

It was the *please* that did it.

"One, I was *never* engaged to your brother. I was contracted to be engaged and married at a later date, which was never specified. Not exactly good contract negotiations," she criticized King Fedir. "So, I *could* have been dating all along."

Heck, she could have been sleeping around. She'd had no legal or moral obligation to go to her marriage bed a virgin, and the stipulation of her chastity or lack of romantic social life until the marriage had not even been alluded to in the contract.

She'd read it through, all thirty-six pages of it, before embarking on the dating article.

"But you did not date before this." Nikolai's words made it very clear that his family had in fact had her watched.

She shrugged, not particularly caring that a *lady* was never supposed to be so dismissive. "I did not want to risk developing an emotional attachment that would have made keeping my promise difficult, or possibly even impossible."

Nikolai nodded in approval of her words. "Very wise."

"So, by converse, you consider that your brother has been foolish?" she asked, unable to resist.

Konstantin cursed.

Nikolai looked at his brother and then back to her. "Considering the outcome of his choices, I would say that is a given."

"My choices?" Konstantin demanded with umbrage. "I was doing my best to protect and expand the business interests of our country so that we did not lose our independent status. How does that make me the bad guy here?"

Nataliya might have agreed with Konstantin, except for two things. One, he'd had affairs, if not dates. Two, he'd acted like an ass about *her* innocent dating.

If he hadn't, she might have even felt compelled to honor the contract.

But Nikolai ignored him. "You said *one*, there are other things wrong with my question?"

"Second, it is obvious that what prompted my actions was my desire *not* to marry a man who so obviously had no more personal integrity than my father."

"I am not like your philandering father." The Prince took clear offence with the comparison. "We were not engaged!"

Nataliya looked at Konstantin with a frown. "If that is your attitude, then how do you explain refusing to marry me because I *dated* other men while you were having *sex* with other women?"

Konstantin's mouth opened and closed without him saying anything.

"Anything else?" Nikolai asked her.

"Do you believe that waiting ten years to fulfill the terms of a contract is keeping good faith in that contract?" she asked instead of answering.

"There were circumstances," Nikolai reminded her, almost gently.

She nodded in agreement. "Your father's heart attack, followed by your own ascension to the throne and your brother having to take over more business responsibility."

"Yes."

"That was eight *years* ago."

"Our family was in mourning," Konstantin said snidely. "Surely you did not expect a formal announcement during that time."

He was referring to the death of his brother's wife, the new Queen, and trying to make her feel small doing it, but Nataliya wasn't going to let anyone in this room make her feel less than. *She* wasn't the one who had dismissed finer feelings or responsibilities.

"It is customary to observe a period of mourning for one year."

And it had been five. It didn't need to be said. They all knew. Again, the timing did not justify the ten-year wait.

For her, or her mother.

"No one from Volyarus approached me about formalizing the engagement," Konstantin pointed out, like that was some kind of fact in his favor.

"Are you saying that you only fulfill the terms of a contract when you are pushed into doing so?" she asked, not impressed and letting that show.

Konstantin glowered. "You have all but admitted you don't want the marriage," he accused rather than answer her question.

She wouldn't deny it. "I do not." While she'd never actually *wanted* to marry this man, she had wanted Mama to be able to return to the bosom of her family.

Nataliya had come to realize both she and her mom were better off without a family that could eject them from their lives so easily, but that was not how it had been ten years ago.

"If you had realized you didn't want to marry my son, surely you should have taken less scandalous steps to insure it." Prince Evengi sounded more baffled than angry at this point. "You could simply have reneged on the contract."

She cast a glance at her uncle before answering. "I approached King Fedir with my desire to do just that."

"And?"

"And he threatened to remove financial support of my mother."

"You are not worried he will do that now?" Nikolai asked her with a frowning side glance toward King Fedir.

"He could try, but I think everyone in this room is aware of how far *I* am willing to go to protect her."

"Are you threatening me, child?" King Fedir asked her, sounding more hurt than worried.

She gave him a cool look, hoping it conveyed just how very little she cared about his hurt feelings after all he had put her mother through. "I am telling you that all actions have consequences and I guarantee you do not want to live with the ones that would come from you doing something so reprehensible."

"Solomia, talk to your daughter!" King Fedir demanded, his shock palpable.

"I am very proud of you, Nataliya, you know that, yes?"

"Yes."

The King frowned. "That is not what I meant."

"You are upset because she carries the ruthlessness that is such a strong trait in our family?" Mama asked her cousin, their King.

Nikolai looked at Nataliya, his expression assessing. "But you did make a promise. *You* signed that contract," Nikolai said.

"I did." Nataliya could wish she hadn't been so eager to *make up* for her father's sins at eighteen, but she couldn't deny she had signed the contract.

"And you take your own promises very seriously."

"I do." Hence her need to get Prince Konstantin to back out of the contract.

Nataliya might no longer feel it was her responsibility to compensate for her father's behavior, but she still understood duty only too well. And she may have been exiled, but her integrity as a member of the royal family was still very much intact.

"She was willing to renege on the contract," Konstantin pointed out. "Her personal ethics cannot be that strong."

King Fedir drew himself up, his expression forbidding. "On the contrary, my *niece* came to me and asked me to negotiate different terms, sure that if the suggestion came from me, you would be more than willing to do so. At no time did she intimate our family should simply *renege*."

Nataliya didn't know what the point was of her cousin harping on how he thought of her as a niece. She would have thought King Fedir would want to distance himself from her at this point. Just as he'd done fifteen years ago.

Nikolai nodded his understanding. "But you refused?"

"I did, more the fool I."

Personally, Nataliya agreed with him. Her uncle had been a fool to think that she would sit meekly by, when in her estimation, she should never have been asked to sign the darn thing in the first place.

"But we raised a lot of money for Mama and Aunt Oxana's favorite charity," she pointed out, not entirely facetiously.

The charity that helped families stay near their children receiving treatment for cancer and other life-threatening illnesses was very dear to Nataliya's heart,

as well. However, no one else seemed to find that the
benefit she did, if all the gloomy faces were to go by.

"All that aside, you still consider yourself bound by
the terms of the contract, do you not?" Nikolai asked
her.

She stared at him, not sure what he was trying to
get at. "Prince Konstantin has verbally repudiated his
willingness to abide by its terms in front of witnesses."

"He did."

She smiled, relief that the current King of Mirrus
wasn't going to try to push her to marry his brother
despite either of their desires.

"The contract, as it is written, still stands," Nikolai
said, his tone brooking no argument.

Shock made Nataliya lightheaded as dread filled her.
"Your brother denounced the contract," she reminded
him, even though she shouldn't have to, because Nikolai had just agreed that was the case. "I am under no
obligation to marry him now."

"But you *are* under obligation to marry a prince of
the House of Merikov," Nikolai said implacably.

Gasps sounded, his father demanded what he meant,
but Nikolai ignored it all, his attention focused entirely
on Nataliya.

Her brain was whirling, trying to parse out what
he meant. Her gaze skittered to the youngest Merikov
Prince. Dimitri, called Dima by his friends of which
she counted herself one, though they'd met on only a
few occasions, they had chatted more via text and email
than she had with Konstantin in past years.

Not even out of the university yet, Dima was looking with utter horror at his eldest brother.

"I will not enter into such a bargain with a child," Nataliya vowed, knowing being called a child would prick her friend and unable to pass up the chance to tease him.

"You were four years younger when you signed that contract ten years ago," Nikolai pointed out without correcting her use of the term *child*, earning a frown from Dima.

"And still desperate to return home. I'm not that teenager any longer either." And she would not allow done to Dima, what had been done to her. She *liked* the twenty-two-year-old Prince.

"Regardless of what your reasons were for signing the contract, you did so. And while you were only eighteen, you were not a minor. You are obligated to its terms unless both parties agree to different ones."

"I will not marry either of your brothers."

"I am glad you did not include me in that categorical refusal." His smile was more like an apex predator baring its teeth.

CHAPTER TWO

"You?" Nataliya asked faintly.

No, Nikolai could not be saying what Nataliya thought he was saying. "You're not a prince." The contract stipulated a prince. "You're a king," her voice rose and cracked on the word *king*, but seriously…?

He had to have lost his mind.

Ten years ago, she would have jumped at the chance to marry this man, but he had only had eyes for the beautiful socialite he had ended up married to. Naively believing that marriage to his brother would cure Nataliya of her adolescent feelings for the unattainable Crown Prince, she'd signed that stupid, bloody, awful contract in good faith.

"But you were married." To the beautiful, sophisticated woman who had become his Queen. Perfect for him in every way, she'd died tragically in a skiing accident. Only later had anyone realized the new Queen had been pregnant at the time.

"And left a widower five years ago."

A widower who would always love the wife he had lost. The fact that he had shown no interest in another woman since the young Queen's death showed that.

Nataliya could not imagine a less appealing marriage to her.

"But..." She didn't know what to say. This was insane.

"You cannot want to marry this woman," Nikolai's father said, voicing Nataliya's own thoughts.

And probably the thoughts of everyone else in the room.

Only Demyan was nodding and Maksim looked satisfied. King Fedir looked astounded. Queen Oxana looked enigmatic, like always. But Nataliya's mom? She looked worried. And that, more than anything, solidified the sense of impending doom settling over Nataliya.

Her *mom* thought he was serious.

"I cannot?" Nikolai asked imperiously.

"She's made a spectacle of herself with that ridiculous article and the accompanying blog posts." Prince Evengi almost looked apologetic in the glance he cast at her. "She's dated no less than ten men, that we know of!"

"She has not had sex with any of them."

"How can you know that?" Prince Evengi asked.

But Nataliya wanted to know too. She *hadn't* had sex with any of them. Or anyone at all. But how could Nikolai know that?

She'd made sure that even if she was being followed by someone on behalf of the House of Merikov, like Demyan had kept tabs on Prince Konstantin, circumstances would be ambiguous enough that no one could be certain. She'd let two of her dates stay the night.

On the sofa, but they hadn't left her apartment until morning.

So, there was no way he could *know* she hadn't had sex.

Only he seemed arrogantly sure of himself.

King Nikolai gave her a measuring look before returning his regard to his father. "Because her integrity would not allow her to do so when the contract is still in place."

"You heard her—she doesn't consider the contract a deterrent," Prince Konstantin said derisively.

"She knows *you* didn't consider it such—that does not mean she has not."

"You expected me to be celibate the last decade?" Konstantin asked, shocked.

Before Nikolai answered, the old King cleared his throat meaningfully. "This is not the place, or time, for this discussion." He turned to his eldest son. "You are not obligated to fulfill the contract on behalf of your brother."

"On that, I do not agree."

And something became very clear to Nataliya, besides the fact that being spoken about like she wasn't there was *extremely* annoying. But this man had an entirely different code of ethics and standard of integrity than his brother.

In truth, Nataliya had never doubted it, but then she'd always thought the best of the man who had become King to save his father's life. The man who she had fallen in love with at age fifteen and had only stopped pining for when she was about twenty.

Funnily enough, it had been his wife's death that had

finally severed Nataliya's unrequited yearning. She'd hurt for him. Grieved from afar on his behalf at the loss of his beloved wife and unborn child and somewhere in the grief, she'd been able to put away her own longing.

It had just felt so selfish. So wrong.

"I can't marry you," she said in a voice much weaker than her normal assertive certainty.

"Oh, but you can, and you will."

The room erupted into pandemonium.

Even Queen Oxana voiced her disbelief at the turn of events.

But Nikolai? Just sat there, looking immovable.

"The contract stipulates a prince of your house," Nataliya reminded him, ignoring everyone else. "You cannot insist I fulfill it by marrying you."

"I was a prince when you signed it, therefore the terms referred to me equally to my brothers."

"No. That's not right."

He just looked at her.

Suddenly, Queen Oxana stood and put her hand out to Nataliya. "That is enough discussion on this topic for present. You and your mother can join me in my apartments."

Nataliya might have argued, but her mother stood and somehow she found herself swept out of the reception room between the two women.

"I can't believe they made you sign that contract!" Gillian, wife to Crown Prince Maksim, exclaimed. "You were just a baby."

"I was eighteen."

"Too young to sign your life away."

"Welcome to life in the royal family," Nataliya said.

She'd left Mama and Oxana to themselves, knowing the two women needed to have a talk that had been fifteen years coming, and had searched out Gillian and her adorable children, finding them taking advantage of the summer sunshine in the palace gardens.

Nataliya loved watching the children play, knowing that the *normalcy* surrounding this very royal family was all down to Gillian's influence.

Gillian frowned, her expression going rock stubborn. "My children will be forced into that kind of agreement over my dead body. They won't be making any decisions about marriage until they are mature enough to do so."

"And when might that be?" Maksim asked drolly as he walked up. "When they are fifty?"

"If they aren't ready to make the decision before then, then yes!" Oh, Gillian was mad. "It's despicable that Nataliya was pressed into signing away her life at such a young age."

On Nataliya's behalf. And Nataliya couldn't say that didn't feel good.

Even her beloved mother had wanted her to sign that contract ten years ago.

Maks looked at Nataliya, something like apology in his brown eyes. "I offered to renegotiate the contract on more favorable terms for Mirrus Global if your participation could be removed from it."

"And?" Gillian demanded when Nataliya remained silent.

"His Highness refused. He considers it a point of family honor for him to fulfill the contract. He's livid with both his father and his brother for the way they spoke to you."

"So, he doesn't agree with the whole misogynistic double standard?" Gillian asked, having gotten the whole story from Nataliya.

"No. He says that neither Nataliya, nor Konstantin were under constraint not to date before a formal engagement was announced."

"Nice of him to absolve his brother too," Nataliya couldn't help saying.

"Did *you* expect him to be celibate?" Maks asked, sounding like he thought it was unlikely.

"I was," Nataliya reminded him.

Maks opened his mouth, but Gillian forestalled him. "Think very hard before you speak again, Maks, because my respect for *your* integrity is on the line here."

He stared at his wife, like he couldn't believe she'd said that.

"I know you are arrogant, but are you seriously going to try to say that Nataliya should have been happy to live in limbo while Prince Konstantin was not?"

"No. That's not what I was going to say at all. I agreed with King Nikolai that neither Nataliya, nor his own brother were under constraints not to date."

"But if I had slept around, what would you have said?" Nataliya couldn't help asking.

Maks's mouth twisted wryly. "That would have depended on the results, wouldn't it?"

"What do you mean?" Nataliya asked.

Maks looked to where the children played, a soft smile curving his usually firm mouth. "Our firstborn child is testament to how unexpected results can come from a night of passion."

"And if the little surprise had been the result of one of Konstantin's many…" Nataliya paused, unsure what term she wanted to use.

Indiscretion implied that Konstantin shouldn't have been having sex with those women. And she wasn't sure she wanted to imply that.

She only knew she didn't want to marry a man who had had so many sexual partners during the ten years he had not made any move to fulfill the terms of the contract they had both signed. Whether Konstantin liked it, or not, to Nataliya, that indicated a man who was both a womanizer and who did not keep his promises. Like her father.

"Sex partners?" Gillian offered, bringing a gasp of outrage from her royal husband.

Gillian rolled her eyes. "Don't be a prude, Maks."

"You are a princess now, Gillian. Maybe you could remember that."

"And this is the twenty-first century. Maybe *you* could remember *that*."

Nataliya found herself grinning despite the stress of the day. "She's got your number, Maks."

"And does King Nikolai have yours?"

"What do you mean?"

"He's completely convinced that you will adhere to the contract."

She didn't want to admit that he might be right. Integrity and honor were every bit as important to her as they were to the King of Mirrus. "I just don't understand why he's saying he wants to marry me."

"Well, he has to marry again at some point," Maks pointed out prosaically.

"But *me*?"

"Perhaps, I could answer that." Nikolai's voice hit Nataliya in the center of her being.

She spun and found him watching her with an implacability that sent a shiver through her.

"I wish you would. This idea that you have to fulfill the contract in place of your brother is ridiculous."

His enigmatic regard turned forbidding. "My honor is not a matter for ridicule."

"But it's not *your* honor in question."

Satisfaction gleamed in his steely gray gaze. "So, you acknowledge that it *is* a matter of honor."

"Prince Konstantin was the Prince referred to in that contract. Everyone knows that," she said, sidestepping the honor issue.

The King settled quite casually onto the fountain rim beside where Nataliya sat. "But it was not in fact, my brother who signed the contract."

"Why wasn't it?" She'd been required to sign on her own behalf and had only noticed that the former King had signed it on behalf of his son, when she'd read it before embarking on her dating campaign.

"In contracts of that sort, it is quite natural for the reigning sovereign to sign on behalf of his house. When I was crowned King, all promises made by my father in matters of state became mine to fulfill."

"So, renegotiate the contract." He had just said he had the power to do so.

"After leaving you and your mother's lives in limbo for ten years? I think not."

"But I don't mind."

"I do."

"I'm not queen material."

"If you marry me, you will be a princess. The title of Queen is bestowed only at my will."

And of course the wife he didn't love wouldn't be worthy of the title, not like the woman he had married and lost. "You know what I mean."

"But I do not agree."

"I'm a computer programmer, not a princess."

"You are a member of the royal family of Volyarus."

Like she needed reminding. "Not so you would notice. Not for the last fifteen years."

Maks made a sound of disagreement, but Nataliya just gave him a look. "When your father exiled me and my mom for my dad's indiscretions, we effectively lost our family. It's no use pretending anything different."

"Nevertheless, you *are* of royal blood, a lady in your own right," Nikolai pressed.

"No one calls me Lady Nataliya." At least no one in her current life.

"I'm sure that's not true. Protocol is observed here in the castle."

"I don't spend time here."

"And yet here you are."

"To answer for crimes that were not in fact crimes at all."

His smile did not reach his eyes. "No, not crimes, but you knew exactly what you were doing when you embarked on that article."

"It was for a perfectly respectable fashion magazine, not a scandal rag."

He nodded. "Well written and the tie in with fashion that you do not in fact have a great deal of interest in was clever."

"My friend thought so."

"Your friend?"

"The contributing editor who wrote the article and blog posts."

"I wondered how you had arranged the article."

"Jenna wanted to do the article but she's in a committed relationship, so she couldn't do the dates."

"Commendable."

"I thought so."

"Yes, you would."

"What is that supposed to mean?" she asked belligerently.

He spread his hands in a gesture of no offense. "You are a woman of definite integrity. Your standards for acceptable behavior match my own."

"How can you say that?" she asked, shocked by how he viewed her. "I hack computers for a living."

"But not for nefarious purposes or your own gain."

"No, of course not." What did he think, she was a criminal?

No, she realized. It was that very certainty that she had *standards* that made her appealing to him.

"Plenty of women who would love to be a princess have integrity," she pointed out dryly.

"But you are the one who signed a contract promising to marry a prince of my house."

"But you aren't a prince."

"We've been over this."

"I just don't understand how you can say you want to marry me."

"Ten years ago, you were vetted and found acceptable."

"For your brother!"

"For any prince of the House of Merikov. That was the way the contract was written."

"That's not how I read it."

"It is standard language for such a contract," Maks pointed out, almost apologetically.

"But that's draconian." Gillian sounded shocked.

Neither the Crown Prince or the King looked particularly bothered by that condemnation.

Nikolai brushed the strands of hair away that the gentle wind had blown across Nataliya's face. She wondered if he even realized he'd done it, but she'd noticed. To the very core of her, a place she'd thought dormant.

Nataliya no longer thought about him *that* way.

But the simple act of him sitting down beside her, close enough she could feel the heat of his body, sparked undeniable sexual desire.

She realized he was watching her as the silence stretched. One of the children started to cry and both Maks and Gillian went over.

Nataliya and Nikolai weren't alone, but it felt like they were.

"You agreed that you signed the contract in good faith." His words didn't register at first.

She was too busy staring into his gorgeous gray eyes, but then her brain caught up with her mouth and she said, "And your brother reneged in front of witnesses today."

"But not on behalf of our house, only himself."

Nataliya surged to her feet. "I'm not eighteen any-more—no one is pushing me into fulfilling that darn contract."

"If you are the woman I believe you to be, you will convince yourself of the rightness of doing your duty."

"To marry you?" she asked in disbelief that simply would not go away.

"To marry me."

"Good luck."

His smile was even more dangerous this time. "I never leave anything to chance."

Ignoring manners and protocol, she turned on her heel and headed back into the palace without another word.

A blooming orchid with tiny buds indicating more flow-ers to come was sitting on the table in her room when she reached it. Nataliya stopped and stared.

What was this?

She picked up the card sitting beside it and felt a shiver go down her spine at the slashing writing.

With my compliments, Nikolai.

In his own hand. Not typed like the ones she'd had delivered from Konstantin.

She recognized the orchid too, from the very dis-tinctive pot it was planted in. She'd been to the castle in Mirrus for the funeral of Nikolai's wife.

There was an orchid room where his mother used to grow the plants, now overseen by a world-renowned horticulturist. All of the orchids in that room were

planted in the same style of pot with the Merikov crest
in fine gold against the eggshell white of the ceramic.

Nataliya had spent a great deal of time in the orchid
room during her three-day stay at the castle five years
before. And she had learned that every orchid growing there had a special history and most were incredibly rare specimens.

Nikolai had caught her there more than once, because as he'd told her, he found comfort in the room
his mother had spent so much time in.

Nataliya had offered to leave, but the young King had
refused, asking her to keep him company. And that's
what she'd done, sitting in silence with a man who was
grieving the loss of his wife and unborn child.

Nataliya could not make sense of the orchid being
here. As gifts went, it was very special. But he couldn't
know that she'd started growing orchids after that visit.
Nothing nearly so impressive as the Merikov collec-
tion, but lovely plants that gave her peace and joy caring for them.

Even if he had known something almost no one else
did, Nikolai could not have gotten the plant delivered
since the recent confrontation. Not even with a helicopter or the palace's personal jet.

Nikolai couldn't have known he planned to take his
brother's place before the meeting today, so why the
orchid?

Whatever the reason, the plant was beautiful and
she knew how very special it was that he'd given it to
her. She grabbed her phone and texted the number no
one but his closest family and advisors was supposed
to have.

Thank you for the orchid. It's beautiful.

His reply came back only seconds later.

I'm glad you like it, my lady. It was one of my mother's favorites.

Why did that *my* feel like it should be bolded? Like he was staking claim? And his assertion this had been one of his mother's plants? How was Nataliya supposed to feel about that?

Special. She felt special. And that was very, very dangerous.

Nataliya had the very distinct feeling that if the King decided to court her, it was going to be a different prospect than the past two months' worth of impersonal gifts sent via Konstantin's staff.

Nataliya remembered that fleeting thought a week later when she looked up from her computer to the sight of Demyan looking amazed.

It was not a look she'd ever seen on her imposing cousin's features before.

Needing a chance to come to terms with Nikolai's demand she fulfill the contract, *with him*, Nataliya had left Volyarus on her cousin's private plane before dinner the night of the big confrontation.

She'd been really grateful that Maks hadn't even blinked at putting his plane at her disposal. He'd assured her that he would smooth things over with his father and their royal visitors.

"You're still my family, Nataliya, and I can only

apologize for not realizing that the exile to America was not voluntary on your mother's part. Had I known I would have redressed the issue."

She'd stared at him. "You were like my big brother. I thought you didn't care."

"My father told me that you and your mother needed space and distance to overcome the humiliation from your father. I believed him."

And then Nataliya had found herself being hugged by her cousin for the first time in over a decade and it had been all she could do not to break down and cry.

Demyan had come to her to say much the same thing when he got back from Volyarus, adding that he'd never stopped considering her a close member of his family.

Now he stood there, with a really weird expression on his face.

"What?" she demanded.

"You got a new computer."

"So?" She hadn't asked Demyan for new hardware though.

"It's from King Nikolai."

Well, that was…*different*. "He gave me a computer." Demyan nodded.

"Why do you look so weird?" she demanded.

"It's a prototype. Even I couldn't get my hands on this build with the new chipset."

That stopped her. "How did you know?"

"Because I had to sign an NDA just to take possession and you've got one to sign too. The company rep is waiting in the conference room."

This was crazy, but she couldn't pretend she wasn't excited. She *loved* new technology and like Demyan had said, this was something even he hadn't been able to finagle out of the manufacturer before early release.

There wasn't just one computer waiting for her in the conference room. There were two. The second was top of the line of available technology and came with a note. *Raise some more money for a very worthy cause.*

Okay, she was impressed. Not just that he'd chosen a gift she would love, her own prototypical, super-slim, ultrafast laptop, but because he'd seen what no one else had. How much she'd enjoyed raising money for the charity she'd chosen. And he was telling her, he wasn't intimidated by the idea she would auction off his gifts.

He expected it. But he provided gifts *to* auction. Over the next two weeks, every gift she received from him came with a personally written note and some kind of duplicate or equivalent item for her to put in the online charity auction.

He also texted her, several times throughout the day. Some innocuous texts. Some even funny. Others surprising, like when he asked her opinion of Dima's desire to take a gap year between university and graduate school. Apparently, when Prince Evengi abdicated his rule to his son, he'd abdicated all major family decisions, as well.

And then there were the texts that drove her batty.

How many children do you want?

Do you object to living in the palace after we marry?

As if her agreement was a foregone conclusion. It annoyed her, but there was this tiny frisson of excitement too. Nikolai was a really special guy and he wanted to marry her.

She knew he wasn't emotionally attached in any way, wasn't even sure if he found her sexually desirable, but he definitely hadn't backed down on his stance.

She knew his father wasn't happy about it. Konstantin wasn't happy. Demyan had told her, and he'd heard it from Maks. But Nikolai was a king and a king who apparently wasn't going to let anyone else dictate his future.

Not like he was doing his best to dictate hers, Nataliya reminded herself.

When the couture gown, shoes, jewelry and handbag arrived along with its auction equivalent and an invitation to dinner and a play two days hence, Nataliya could do nothing but stare in consternation at the boxes littering her desk.

Demyan stood, leaning against the doorjamb. "So, he's finally moving this courtship into the dating stage."

"Can you date a king?" she asked, a tinge of hysteria touching her voice.

"I guess you're going to find out."

"He thinks that stupid contract has me all sewn up."

"No, he thinks your sense of duty and integrity has you all sewn up. But give the guy his due, he's setting the rest of his life up to fulfill his own sense of honor."

"I know you think duty is all there is to life—"

"Not since I married Chanel, but I won't pretend duty didn't play a big part in that."

"And that duty nearly destroyed your marriage." She'd been invited to the wedding. She'd seen the other woman's reaction before Chanel had disappeared from the reception without her groom.

And frankly, Nataliya had known all along what was going on. She was nosy and she had more ways than most of finding out what she wanted to know.

"We all make sacrifices for family and the good of Volyarus."

And she knew that despite how close he'd come to losing his wife, Demyan still saw duty in all capitals when he thought about it. Chanel just made sure that there was more to his life than a single concept.

"I made my sacrifice ten years ago, to provide a way for my mother to return home."

"And now she no longer wants to return to Volyarus full-time."

"But my sacrifice is still there, hanging over my head."

"Maybe it won't turn out to be such a sacrifice after all."

He could say that. Demyan's own sacrifice had led to the love of his life and children he adored. Hers could lead nowhere but heartache. Nikolai would never love her as he'd loved his first wife and even if she no longer felt the same things for him she once had, Nataliya didn't want to be trapped in a marriage to a man whose heart was locked in the past.

CHAPTER THREE

NATALIYA WAS NOT at all surprised when her phone dinged with a text ten minutes before the limo was supposed to arrive for her.

Nikolai had texted updates on his schedule and arrival throughout the day.

Like he wanted to make sure she was ready, like he worried she might get the time wrong, or something. Or maybe, he just wanted to be sure she was going to show up. After all, not once had he actually asked her to join him for dinner and the play. No, just the delivery of the dress and tickets which she doubted very sincerely they would have to show to take their seats.

She had no doubt that between him and his security detail, they were taking up an entire box at the theater.

As a king, he was used to getting his way. And she'd been, oh, so tempted to simply not be here tonight, but the truth was, she and Nikolai needed to talk.

Nataliya needed him to understand that his honor would not be compromised by renegotiating the contract.

A sharp knock sounded at the door and Nataliya smoothed the opalescent gray designer dress down her long body. She had to admit that Nikolai had good taste in women's fashion. Though considering the perfectly coiffed fashionista he'd been married to, Nataliya should not be surprised.

"Showtime," said Jenna, her friend who had written the "50 First Dates for a Would-Be Princess" article.

She'd come over today to help Nataliya prep for her date with a king, doing Nataliya's makeup and hair, styling her so that Nataliya looked better than she had for any of those first dates.

Because Nataliya had not wanted to look like a consolation date in any of the pictures that were bound to be taken by the paparazzi.

Not because she wanted to try to look her best for Nikolai.

Nataliya opened the door to her condo and stepped back in shock that the King stood on the other side, two of his security detail hovering in the background. The others were no doubt securing the building.

"You didn't need to come up," she said, unable to hide her surprise at his presence.

Wearing a light custom-made charcoal gray suit that accentuated his six-foot-four, well-muscled frame, his presence sent a hurricane rioting through her senses.

Every part of her body suddenly felt more alive, more *present* and it was hard to take each new breath.

"May I come inside?"

She jolted, realizing she was letting the King of Mirrus stand in the hall like a salesman. "Of course."

Nataliya stepped back and he followed her inside, one of his security men accompanying him to do a routine sweep of her condo while the other pulled the door shut behind them to stand at attention on the other side.

Neither Demyan, nor Maks practiced such heavy security protocols when they were in Seattle.

But then, Nikolai was a king already, despite being only thirty-five years old.

"The dress looks every bit as beautiful on you as I thought it would." He took her in, his gray eyes going molten with an expression she had never expected to see in his eyes.

Desire.

"Thank you." She swallowed. "You could have sent a car for me to meet you at the restaurant."

Who had ever heard of a king calling for his date in person?

She'd made the mistake of telling him how impersonal and detached she'd considered his brother's overtures. And Nikolai had assured her, his would not be.

But seriously? Could he say *overkill*?

"Surely not." He reached out and brushed a proprietary finger along her collarbone. "This will be our first public appearance together. Calling for you at your door is only the most basic courtesy."

Heat whooshed through her body from that one small touch and Nataliya was momentarily unable to respond.

"Well, I'm impressed," Jenna said forthrightly.

Nikolai turned to acknowledge the other woman. "Jenna Beals, former college roommate and good friend of my intended as well as contributing editor for the fashion forward magazine that ran the article on my future betrothed, I believe."

Jenna gave a credible curtsy. "It's a pleasure to meet you, Your Highness."

Nikolai smiled, his gray eyes warm. "I liked the article and blog posts."

"You did?" Jenna asked in clear shock. "Really?"

"It was a clever concept, showing the fashion side of the modern dating game."

Jenna gave Nataliya a significant look. "He doesn't think you should be shamed for going out on a few dates."

"Not at all, but all future dates will be with me," he said with arrogant assurance.

"Because you have so much time to spend with me," Nataliya said with unhindered cynicism.

"And yet, here I am."

"But this is a one-off." Wasn't it? He was a king, he didn't have time to woo her.

Woo. What an old-fashioned word, but what else fit?

His honor demanded he fulfill the contract on behalf of his family and he was determined to convince her that marriage to him was what she wanted. Ten years ago, it wouldn't have taken any convincing.

But that was then and this was now.

The multi-Michelin-star restaurant he took her to for dinner was one she'd heard a lot about, but had never tried. The simple, elegant modern Japanese-style decor went perfectly with the Asian Fusion food on offer.

Among the diners on the way to their table, she recognized two prominent politicians, a football star and a television star.

Even the notable patrons' attention caught on King

Nikolai and his entourage as they walked through the restaurant. Security took tables on either side of the one she and Nikolai were led to.

He held her chair for her, himself, his closeness impacting her in ways something so simple should not have.

Disconcerted, she blurted, "You don't have to do this over-the-top stuff. I'm a computer programmer, not a princess."

"You are Lady Nataliya and when we are wed, you will be The Princess of Mirrus."

"As opposed to *a* princess?"

He settled into his own seat across from her at the intimate table for two. "It is the distinction given to the wife of the King."

"I haven't said I'm going to marry you," she said quietly, not wanting to be overheard.

The expression on his chiseled features was untroubled. "On the contrary, you signed a contract that said that very thing."

She looked around and though no one was looking at them, that did not mean none of the other diners were listening. Though the acoustics in the restaurant and table placement made it unlikely.

"Why?" she asked him.

"Why?" He paused. "What?"

"You know what I'm asking. You turned down Maks's offer to renegotiate the contract at favorable terms for Mirrus Global."

"But I do not wish to renegotiate the contract. There are not terms more favorable than the ones we have now."

He could not mean what it sounded like he meant, that marriage to *her* was the most favorable term.

"You can't want to marry me." This she whispered nearly inaudibly, paranoid about being overheard as only the daughter of the notorious Count Shevchenko could be.

"You are mistaken."

That was all. *You are mistaken.* No explanation, but then this was not the place to have this conversation.

She should have brought it up in the limousine, but she'd been fighting entirely adult sexual feelings she had never experienced before. And he'd been happy to keep up the conversation with a charming urbanity that only increased his attractiveness to her.

Not one of the fourteen men she'd dated so far for the article and its accompanying blog posts had been even remotely as interesting, even the computer programmer who had developed an app that she loved to use.

"I am still obligated to go on thirty-six dates for the article," she apprised him, surprised at her own reticence about doing so.

"Thirty-five." His smile was way too appealing for her peace of mind.

"Thirty-five?"

"Tonight is one."

"But the photos of my style." That was the whole point of the article.

And technically, it *could* work, because Jenna *had* styled her.

"I will take care of it." He called one of his security people over with a jerk of his head.

A few low-spoken words and the other man went back to his table, his phone already out.

"A photographer will be here before we are finished with our dinner."

"I'm sure Jenna will appreciate that." Because honestly? Nataliya had made up sixteen different excuses for not scheduling a date the past two weeks.

"I will make sure we have a photographer on hand for the remainder of our dates."

"You're not going to take me out thirty-five more times." No way did he have the time.

"Some of those dates will have to happen after our wedding, but I fail to see why you are so surprised at the idea. You did not imagine that we would lead separate lives?"

"What do you mean *after* our wedding? When do you think we are getting married?" It took at least a year, usually two, to plan a royal wedding.

"Three months from now Mirrus is hosting a summit for small countries and monarchies. I would like the event to culminate in our wedding."

"Maks and Gillian did that, but she was pregnant. There was a reason for the rush."

He tilted his dark head in acknowledgment. "You have waited ten years for my house to fulfill its part of that contract. That is long enough."

"You're really stuck on this honor-of-your-house thing, aren't you?"

She expected him to get angry, or at least annoyed, by her snark.

But Nikolai smiled. "Yes, in fact, I am."

She sighed, acknowledging if only to herself, that

he would not be manipulated as easily as his brother.

"You're not going to be reasonable about this, are you?"

"If by reasonable, you mean change my mind, no."

She felt her own usually even temper rising. "You do realize you are a king, right?"

"And as such, I am accustomed to getting my own way."

She'd just been thinking that very thing, but still. "You're not supposed to admit that."

"I should lie?" he asked arrogantly.

"I don't know. Can you really see me as your Queen? Excuse me... I mean your Princess?"

"I have no trouble picturing that eventuality at all." The expression in his eyes was all male approval.

And it did something to her insides she did not want to admit. "I don't like dressing up."

"Yet you do so very well. I will never be anything but proud to have you stand by my side."

She frowned. He couldn't mean that. "I blurt stuff out before I think about it," she warned him.

"Do you? Thus far, I've noticed you being very careful about what you say and where you say it."

That was true in certain circumstances, like the few in which they'd met, but not always. "When I'm comfortable, I lose the filter between my brain and my mouth."

"I will look forward to you growing comfortable with me then."

"You don't mean that." How could he?

He didn't quite smile, but amusement lurked in his usually steely gray gaze. "You think I only want people around me who say what I want to hear?"

"You're a king."

"We've established that."

"You don't like people disagreeing with you."

"Disagreement is healthy." He gave her a look she thought might be intended to intimidate. "Disrespect is something else."

She wasn't intimidated, but she was curious. "What if you think I'm being disrespectful when I'm only being honest?"

"What if you think I'm being neglectful when I am only busy?" he riposted.

"I don't know."

"Neither do I. Marriage requires trust and compromise from both sides."

"Is that what you had with Tiana?"

Nothing changed in his expression, but there was a new quality of stillness about him and rigidity to Nikolai's spine. "My first marriage is not something I like to discuss."

"Okay."

His eyes widened fractionally. "Okay?"

"I don't like talking about my childhood either." Everyone thought they knew what her life had been like because her father had been in the tabloids so much.

No one but she and her mother knew about the Count's violent rages, about the mental and physical scars both she and her mother bore because of them.

His final desertion had embarrassed the royal family and torn their lives apart, but it had also come as a terrible relief. Once they reached the States, her mother had taken out a restraining order against her estranged husband and renewed it after their divorce became final.

Living in the States, she'd finally stood up for herself and her daughter in a way she'd never been willing to do when their lives were wrapped with the Volyarus royal family.

"Hearing you say that makes me very curious, *kiska*."

He could be as curious as the proverbial cat, but she wasn't talking about those dark years when her father had lived with her and Mama in Volyarus.

Not for anything. "I'm not a kitten."

"Oh, I think you are. You've proven you have sharp little claws, but you are not vicious with them and I am very much looking forward to petting you."

She choked on the wine she'd been sipping. "I can't believe you said that."

"I am a king, not a eunuch."

"But you don't want me."

"Don't I?" His heated expression belied her claim.

Suddenly, the air around them was charged and she pressed her thighs together under the table. "I don't look anything like Tiana," Nataliya blurted.

Dark brows raised, he said, "You look like yourself and I find you very attractive."

"Oh." She really hadn't expected that blunt declaration, much less the truth he'd have her believe was behind it. Unexpected heat suffused her face.

"Nothing to say back to me?"

"What do you want me to say?" she asked in a tone that was way too breathless.

"You could tell me if the attraction is one-sided."

"Of course, I'm attracted to you." He was smart, powerful, gorgeous, strong and just downright sexy. "Who wouldn't be?"

"I think I'm flattered." But he didn't sound too sure about that fact.

And for some inexplicable reason, that made Nataliya happy. She didn't like him taking her attraction to him for granted, despite the fact he had to know that most women would find him pretty much irresistible. "Don't be. You know who and what you are."

"Yes, but I was beginning to wonder if *you* appreciated my attributes."

He had to be joking. "I find that hard to believe."

She was no actress and right now, Nataliya couldn't stop thinking how much she wanted to kiss him and try things she'd never tried before with another man. It was all his fault too, the King who talked bluntly about stuff like *attraction*.

Which naturally sent her thoughts in a direction they never went. Except around him. And that had been a long time ago.

Only this was now and although she was no longer in love with him, Nataliya apparently still found Nikolai sexually irresistible.

And the King's expression said he knew it too!

A smile more predatory than amused creased his gorgeous lips. "The look on your face says that our wedding night will be very satisfying."

"Like you'd allow it to be anything else," she blurted with more honesty than common sense. "You're the guy who always wins."

"It comes with the territory."

Satisfied with how their evening had gone so far, Nik slid into the limousine, taking the seat beside his future bride rather than the one across from her.

Although she was more stubborn than he'd given her credit for, Nik had no doubt that she would eventually agree to marry him.

Because Nataliya was that rare commodity in his world—a woman of honor.

When she made a promise, she kept it. Not like the faithless socialite he'd made his Queen. He'd made the mistake once of bestowing political and social power that rivaled his own on his wife and lived to regret it.

Nataliya had waited ten years on a contract that should have been fulfilled in half that time. And she had not allowed herself to consider getting out of her obligation to marry a prince of his house until she had discovered Konstantin's propensity for one-night stands.

Nataliya had very exacting standards and a highly developed sense of honor, both for herself and others. In her view, Konstantin hadn't lived up to those standards.

Nikolai understood, even if he did not agree fully. Her attitude was to his benefit.

And it was those traits that had first made Nik realize she would make his ideal wife. The low-simmering attraction he'd recognized in the agonizing days after his pregnant wife's death was also welcome. He had no desire to have an icy-cold marriage bed, but even he had not realized how deeply that attraction ran until he started spending more time with Nataliya.

He'd even been turned on during the confrontation at the Volyarussian palace.

Not that he would ever acknowledge such a thing.

Nor would ever lose control of his desire or allow it to drive his decisions.

He would not make the same mistakes with his second wife he had made with his first.

Starting with choosing a woman who had bone-deep integrity and absolutely no tolerance for infidelity.

Nataliya allowed Jenna to put the finishing touches to her makeup for the fifth date in three weeks with Nikolai.

He had stayed in Seattle that first week, managing to see her every day he had been in town.

The next week he had flown in to take her to the big technology expo. That would have been amazing enough, especially with the VIP treatment attending it with a king had provided. Yes, even Nataliya in all her pragmatism had been impressed. But somehow he had managed an invite for her to the super-secret hackathon she'd been trying to get into for the last three years.

And the King of Mirrus had not complained even a little when she'd immersed herself in learning new hacking technologies and going up against some of the biggest names in her industry for hours.

Tonight they were attending a fund-raiser ball for the children's charity she'd been donating the proceeds of her *Courtship Gifts for a Would-Be Princess* online auction to.

It was being held at one of the swankest hotels in Manhattan and Nikolai had arranged for a private plane to fly Nataliya, Jenna, the photographer and even Jenna's boyfriend to New York.

Jenna and her boyfriend were excited about going out on the town after Jenna finished styling Nataliya for her date and getting the information the junior fashion editor needed for her blog post.

"My boss is beside herself with joy in the amount of hits we're getting on the blog from this series," Jenna said with satisfaction as she stood back.

Nataliya smiled at her longtime friend. "Good. You deserve recognition for your creativity."

"But it's your life that's making this possible. Everyone is keen to follow the courtship of a king and his would-be princess."

Nataliya was unwillingly enthralled herself. She spent too much time wondering what his next move would be and thinking about him between frequent texts and phone calls. "I think he's still expecting the wedding to take place month after next."

"Has he said so?"

"I got the mock-up invitations to approve this afternoon." But so far, she had not actually agreed to marry him.

He acted like it was a foregone conclusion. Because she'd signed that darned contract.

Jenna tried to stifle laughter but wasn't successful. "He's very confident you're going to agree, isn't he?"

"The word is arrogant."

"I'm pretty sure kings are allowed."

Nataliya smoothed a tiny wrinkle in the skirt of her dress. "And I'm *very* sure that he would be just as arrogant if he were the third son of the King's second cousin."

Jenna's laughter burst out and Nataliya couldn't help joining her, but she hadn't been joking. Not entirely.

Nikolai was always sure he was right and she'd yet

to find an instance in which he was not. She couldn't even deny that she *would* ultimately agree to marry him.

She would like to say that was all due to her sense of duty and the contract she'd signed at the age of eighteen. And she could not deny that it did play a part, but that crush she'd gotten over?

Not so much in the *over* department.

Nikolai treated her like a person in her own right, not just an adjunct to his life. He didn't dismiss her job or put her down for loving what she did. Nor did he criticize her for having no personal clue about the latest fashions or being mostly ignorant of pop culture.

Nataliya wasn't interested in being *seen*, nor did she have any interest in playing on her current A-Lister status as Jenna called it.

Nikolai approved of her and supported Nataliya's interests and opinions in a way even her mom found challenging, Nataliya knew.

She was nobody's idea of perfect royalty.

So why did this King want to marry her?

What could *she* bring to the Royal House of Merikov? Other than her womb.

No question she would be expected to provide heirs *plural* to the throne. He'd been very frank about that fact. Just as he'd been, oh, so open on that first date about being attracted to her.

And yet he hadn't even kissed her. Not once. No kisses, no heated embraces.

Did he expect to use artificial insemination, or something, to get those heirs he was so keen on?

The thought was really lowering, but what else was she supposed to think?

He was so incredibly polite. And she? Wanted to kiss him and try all the things she'd ever read about with him. Sometimes he looked at her with what she thought was desire, but he never acted on it and she couldn't help thinking she'd got it wrong.

But did that stop her wanting him?

No it did not.

Stifling a sigh at her thoughts, Nataliya obediently looked in the mirror to check out Jenna's handiwork.

The dress was from an established design house but far from classic. Black lace over a nude slip that stopped midthigh, one shoulder was entirely bare and the other sleeve reached to her wrist. When she shifted, the slit that went right to the bottom of the slip showed her leg. The cut and style made the slit look like it went higher, but it did not in fact show anything but the pale skin of her thigh.

Thank goodness she did her muscle-toning elliptical every morning, or she would never show so much of her leg.

Biting her lip, Nataliya met Jenna's expectant gaze in the mirror. "It looks so risqué."

"But nothing that shouldn't be showing is."

"You can see the side of my breast."

"No, you think you can but the fashion tape and cut of the gown are both clever enough to keep you covered."

"Nikolai is going to have a fit."

Jenna rolled her eyes. "His Highness has been mixing with the glitterati for years while you've been happily moldering away at your computer keyboard. He's seen much more daring gowns."

More daring? What were they, see-through? When she asked, Jenna just laughed. "It has been known."

"This one looks like it's see-through."

"But it's not."

"The nude slip is an exact match for my skin tone."

"That was done on purpose," Jenna revealed with a tone of pure satisfaction. The clothes being provided by the fashion houses for Nataliya's dates were a serious coup for her friend. "The in-house designers were happy to provide a personalized gown for this event for you. You're an A-Lister now, hon."

"Only because I'm dating a king."

"Um…you do realize you just said that, right?"

Nataliya shook her head, but the image in the mirror was a woman who *could* date a king. Even she knew that. "You did good, friend."

"I had a great canvas to work with."

Now if only Nikolai would not just see Nataliya as a woman who could date a king, but one the said King would want to kiss. And perhaps do other naughty things with, *she* might feel like crowing.

CHAPTER FOUR

NIKOLAI'S INITIAL REACTION was all that Nataliya could have wanted.

Steel-gray eyes turned molten with hot desire and she prepared herself for a kiss to blow her socks off.

Good thing she wasn't wearing any socks because no kiss was forthcoming and the King's expression shuttered almost immediately.

"You look beautiful," he told her, oh, so politely.

And Nataliya wanted to scream. "Thank you," she replied in kind, however, none of the frustration she felt bleeding into her voice.

"Once we are married, however, you will not be styled so provocatively." He gave her another cursory glance before leading her out of the hotel suite. "It is a good thing you are not enamored with this type of fashion. That will not be a loss for you."

Every word he spoke stoked the annoyance simmering inside Nataliya until she felt like a fizzing teakettle.

"*When* we are married?" she asked delicately. "Having you dictate how I dress won't be a hardship for me?" she inquired with even more precise syllables.

He stopped in the elevator, his gaze flicking to the

security detail before coming to settle on her. "Naturally, my opinion on how you dress will be important to you."

"Oh, really?" she asked sweetly. "Because, and I know this is going to come as a surprise to you, but I have been dressing myself for years now and I have never once needed a man's opinion on what *I* choose to wear."

"You will be my Princess, and with that honor will come certain responsibilities," he said repressively, the buttoned-down King she'd gotten to know early on making a full appearance for the first time on one of their dates.

Somehow, with all the worries she'd had about the responsibilities of becoming a princess, none of them had ever centered around her wardrobe. "Responsibilities like letting you tell me how to dress?"

"Be honest—would you have chosen that dress on your own?" he asked, sounding like he knew the answer already.

"I don't wear high-end designer gowns on a regular basis, full stop."

"You could, though, if you wanted. I have never seen your mother wearing anything but."

"She accepts an allowance from her cousin." Hush money Nataliya had no interest in. "I live on the money I earn."

"Admirable, but when you are *The* Princess of Mirrus, you will dress in the top designers' creations and I do not believe that *you* will choose clothing as provocative as the dress you are currently wearing."

She had this crazy urge to wear nothing but sexually provocative clothing for the rest of her life. Comfortable, or not. "Let me make something very clear, Your Highness."

He waited without saying anything, his manners impeccable.

"I will wear the clothes *I* like regardless of who I am married to. That means that if I want to wear jeans from a department store, I will and if I want to wear dresses just like this one, I will. No one, not even a king, is going to dictate my choices like a petty fashion tyrant."

One of the bodyguards made a suspicious sound that could have been humor, but a look at their faces showed only impassive regard.

When Nikolai opened his mouth to speak, his eyes narrowed in clear irritation, she held up her hand.

"I am not finished."

"Then by all means, continue."

"You have not asked me to marry you. We are not engaged and speaking to me like that is a done deal when you haven't even given me the courtesy of that one small tradition is *not* making the outcome you so clearly want more likely." With that she set her not-so-happy gaze on the bodyguard nearest the door. "Open the doors—this discussion is over."

She'd noticed the elevator stopped moving, but the doors had remained shut. His security detail was always one step ahead of any potential problem. She admired that kind of cunning even if right now she wanted off that lift more than just about anything.

A small jerk of his head meant the doors remained closed. "Hardly a discussion when you have not allowed me to speak."

"No, you are right, it is *not* a discussion when the man who intends to marry me, despite having never gotten my agreement to that eventuality, starts laying down the law about the way I will be dressing in the future. I don't remember you asking my opinion on that, you are right."

With that she gave the bodyguard a look letting him know she meant business, but was sure the King had given his tacit approval, or the doors would not have swished open.

Uncaring of the why, Nataliya swept out of the elevator, heading for the front doors, certain their limousine would be waiting for her outside.

They were in the car and moving through city traffic before he broke the silence between them. "It was not my intention to offend you with my remarks."

"Wasn't it? But I'd always believed you were a top-drawer diplomat," she said with no little sarcasm. Just what exactly had he intended if not to offend?

His mouth firmed. "I assumed that certain things had been made clear to you at finishing school as you were supposed to be prepared for eventual marriage to a prince of my house."

"Newsflash, I did not agree with everything my mentors said in finishing school and found the university far more to my liking." In fact, she'd only attended said finishing school so she *could* attend university and pursue a degree in computer programming and software design.

Something even her mother had insisted was unnecessary and would end up being useless to Nataliya later in life. Solomia had wanted her to get a liberal arts degree if Nataliya insisted on going to college. But Nataliya had fought for the future she'd wanted, while believing that part of that future was out of her control and had been since she was eighteen.

"The reports from the school do not mention a tendency to rebellion."

She wasn't at all surprised Nikolai had read Nataliya's progress reports from finishing school. She had no doubt he'd also read her college transcripts and all relevant commentary from professors and teachers alike.

"The fact I became a computer hacker rather than following a far more acceptable pursuit for a future princess didn't enlighten you?" she asked, revising her view of his powers of observation.

And not in a positive direction.

"Funnily enough, no."

"Because I never rebelled against the medieval contract I signed when I was eighteen?" she guessed.

The infinitesimal shift in his expression said she'd got it in one.

"I can't really explain that in terms of my sense of independent thought. It was just there, this knowledge I had promised to marry Konstantin."

"A prince of my house, not Konstantin per se."

"Well, he was the one I thought I was marrying and honestly? I wasn't keen to date or fall for someone and get hurt like Mama had been by my father."

"Theirs was a love match?"

"On her side, though their parents *were* instrumental in bringing them together." And like so many times in her mother's life, it was obvious *her* parents had placed their own social standing and prestige above what was best for their daughter.

Her grandparents hadn't argued against Mama's and Nataliya's exiles any more than anyone else had. Both had died, their daughter never restored to her place of birth.

"So you had family precedent."

"I'm a member of the royal family of Volyarus—of course I had precedent. Aunt Oxana married my uncle to give him heirs and he never let his mistress go. She made marriage for duty look easy." And somehow *right*.

Her aunt had never been *happy* in her marriage. She couldn't have been, but Oxana had never complained, had never shown regret for becoming Queen and giving birth to the heir to the throne.

"Your attitude has changed though?" he asked, not sounding happy.

"Not exactly." She may not have enjoyed finishing school, but Nataliya had been taught from birth to put duty to the royal family first.

She simply intended to do that without losing herself in the process.

She tried to put that into words and was surprised at the understanding that came over the King's features. Not only understanding, but approval.

"You have a strong sense of integrity and duty, but also an equally strong sense of self. Believe it, or not, Nataliya, I think that is a good thing."

"Even if it means I wear provocative couture one day and jeans off the rack the next?"

"It will be *my* preference that my wife dress appropriate to her station on all the days, but how to define that will naturally not only be for me to determine."

She wasn't sure she believed him. The guy who thought he didn't have to *ask* her to marry him despite her spelling it out to him. And she wasn't all that impressed with his belief it was *not only* his to determine, rather than *hers* in full.

Despite the argument that Nikolai insisted on referring to as a lively discussion, Nataliya enjoyed herself very much at the charity ball.

She was thrilled Nikolai had purchased an entire table's worth of tickets and then rather than filling the spots with dignitaries, he'd held a lottery for the employees of the charity to fill the seats. Each seat came along with the privilege of bidding on auction items up to a set amount that the House of Merikov would pay. In every way, he gave the seat winners a fairy-tale evening.

It was brilliant PR, but even with that aspect, she couldn't help being flat-out impressed.

Who wouldn't want to be with the guy so willing to make other people's dreams come true?

In his perfectly tailored dinner suit, he was also the best-looking man in the giant ballroom. She let herself fall into the fantasy as they danced after the auction to music slow enough to justify him holding her.

But the fantasy crashed and burned when a tap on his shoulder indicated another man wanted to break into the dance. That other man? Her father.

She gasped, anger filling her faster than the air refilling her lungs and then she jerked back in involuntary reaction to her father's nearness.

"No." She shook her head. "I am not dancing with you."

"You are making a scene," her father censured her. He gave his patented smile to the King. "Pardon my daughter, she has clearly spent too many years living like a commoner."

Panic tried to claim Nataliya, but she refused to let it take hold. Looking around them, she realized they were the center of attention among the nearest dancing couples. Soon it would be the whole room, but she *would not* dance with her father.

"You will have to excuse us, but I do not enjoy the opportunity of dancing with my intended often enough to relinquish her to another." Nikolai adroitly pulled her back into his arms and shifted so he stood between her and her father.

Shock coursed through her and she nearly stumbled.

No one had ever stood between her and her father. Not once. Not her mother. Not the security detail hired to protect her family, not her royal relatives.

The idea that Nikolai would risk making a scene to back up her refusal to dance with the Count was so astonishing, she had no frame of reference for it.

This was the man who had spent the beginning of their evening making it clear he expected her to dress the part of his Princess and yet when it came to actions, he was not allowing diplomacy to guide him.

But rather her expressed needs.

Her father tapped on the King's shoulder again, his smug smile still in place. "I really must insist. It has been too long since I have seen my daughter."

"No." That was all Nikolai said, but he did it with utter freezing civility and spun her away.

"Do you want me to have my security alert the authorities? Count Shevchenko is breaking the restraining order you and your mother have out against him, is he not?"

"You know about that?" Although when they'd first been exiled, her father had gone to Monaco with his latest flame, he followed Nataliya and her mother to Seattle when he ran out of money.

One trip to the ER later and her mother filed for divorce and the restraining order in the same week.

Her father had settled in New York, unwilling to risk jail time returning to Washington State.

"But apparently no one in your Volyarussian family does."

"Mama doesn't want anyone in her family to know." Her father's violent nature was never to be spoken of to anyone else. Mama had drilled that into Nataliya from her earliest memories.

While Mama had taken the order out and done more to break away from her toxic marriage than she'd ever done in Volyarus, Nataliya's mother felt deep shame for what her husband had done to her and their daughter. Mama had never wanted to talk about it, though she had started seeing a therapist.

Nataliya had learned young to carry the shame of her father's sins as if they were her own.

"Why?" Nikolai asked her.

And it took a moment for Nataliya to order her chaotic thoughts enough to realize what he was asking. "Because she's afraid they'll tell her she's wrong to have filed for it and kept it current? Because she's ashamed we need one? Because one simply does not talk about things like infidelity, much less abuse? Because she was made to feel like she carried the blame as much as he did for his actions? Take your pick."

"As you have been made to feel that his failings are yours?" Nikolai asked far too astutely.

"Does it matter? I know I'm not responsible for his actions."

"Maybe coming to realize that made you less willing to tolerate the claim the contract between our families had on you."

He could be right. Nataliya had grown less willing to play her part as future bride of Prince Konstantin from the time she'd realized she wasn't paying the price for her mother's happiness, but for her father's sins.

Remembering what else Nikolai had asked, she sighed. "No authorities. The order is filed in Washington, not New York. It would be a hassle and he'd talk himself out of it anyway."

"I will not let him near you."

"Why would you promise that?" How could he know that even her father's proximity sparked irrational panic in Nataliya?

"Did you know that he put his last mistress in the hospital?"

She shook her head, feeling guilt that was not hers to feel. Nataliya was not responsible for the actions of her father. Not now. Not in the past.

It had been a difficult lesson to learn, but she'd refused to spend her entire life feeling shame for her father's ugly choices.

"Neither you, nor your mother told your family what he was really like?"

"We were already so ashamed of his public behavior, we couldn't share what he was like at home."

"You were a child. She was the wife he did not honor." Nikolai's tone was certain. "Neither of you had any shame to carry."

"I know that in my head but getting my heart to believe has been a years' long process."

"I did not know he would be here."

"Me either. Do you think he knew I would be?"

Nikolai inclined his head austerely. "Our plans have been of utmost interest to the media."

"It's the fairy-tale story of the decade." Nataliya's mouth twisted cynically. "The King who's courting the lady who lives like a commoner."

"So you acknowledge I *am* courting you."

"I have never denied it."

"You simply refuse to confirm the outcome."

"Have you asked me to?" she asked, working not to roll her eyes.

"You're very much hung up on that issue."

"And you are very arrogant."

He shrugged. "It would be stranger if I was not."

"Haven't you heard? Humility is a trait to be admired."

"False humility has no appeal to me."

She huffed out a laugh, unable to stop herself. "Clearly."

"You think I should pretend not to know my own mind? Where is the integrity in that?"

"No, I don't think you should pretend. I think you should not be so sure you know best all the time."

"But I do."

"Hush. Just dance with me, all right? I've had an upsetting moment."

He pulled her just a little closer while remaining nothing but appropriate in how he held her. "Hushing."

"Do you always have to have the last word?" she asked, exasperated.

He just looked at her, as if saying, *No, see? Here I am not having the last word.*

In that moment, she wanted nothing more than to press her body into his and lay her head on his strong shoulder. Let him hold her and protect her, when she had never expected anyone else to protect her. When her entire life, all Nataliya could remember was doing her best to protect others.

She could still remember being no older than three or four and stepping between her mother and father, yelling at him to stop hitting her mama. He'd backhanded her so hard she'd hit the wall and she could remember nothing else from that night.

She didn't know if she'd been knocked out or it was just her spotty trauma memory at work again, leaving holes that often made little sense to her.

They were in the limousine on the way back to her hotel suite when she commented, "I think my father left early. It's not like him to give up so easily. I was sure he'd try to talk to me again."

"I had him escorted out."

"Aren't you worried he'll go to the press and accuse

you of throwing your weight around?" That was exactly the kind of thing Count Danilo Shevchenko would do.

Nikolai did not look worried. "I think my reputation can withstand anything a disgraced count could attempt to throw at it."

There went his arrogance again, but she admitted she liked it, if only to herself. "I'm sorry."

"You have nothing to apologize for."

"Would you be saying that if I refused to honor the contract?" she couldn't help asking.

"But you are not going to refuse."

"You're so sure." When she still wasn't.

"You have more integrity than any woman I know."

"I know loads of women with integrity."

"As do I, but not one of them is more honorable than you."

"Even Queen Tiana?" She wished she could take the question back the moment it popped out.

He'd said he didn't want to talk about his first marriage. Besides, it made Nataliya sound insecure and she didn't like that.

He surprised her by answering though. "Yes." He looked like he was thinking about what he wanted to say next. "Our marriage was not the perfect joining of two hearts the media painted it to be."

If the fact he'd answered was surprising, the answer itself shocked her. Nataliya remembered how in love he'd seemed when he'd married the daughter of one of the new Russian oligarchy. Nataliya had thought the other woman beautiful but spoiled.

And she'd felt bad for thinking that. She'd always assumed her impression of the other woman was skewed by Nataliya's own unrequited feelings for Nikolai. And she hadn't liked knowing that about herself.

"Thank you," she said now, not sure what else to say in the light of her own nosy question and his very unexpected, honest answer.

He shrugged, but his expression was forbidding. "I was not flattering you, merely speaking the truth."

"Still, it's a nice truth to hear. To be valued for something other than my womb and royal lineage is surprisingly satisfying." She wasn't going to mention the comparison with his dead wife where Queen Tiana came out second.

Or his admission his first marriage hadn't been perfect. That wasn't the important issue here anyway.

"I am glad you think so."

She bit back a sigh. It *was* nice to hear, but could his respect for her make for a strong marriage when he showed no actual desire for her despite having told her he thought she was attractive?

Biting her lip, she studied him and then finally asked. "Are you ever going to kiss me?"

There could be no doubt she'd surprised him. It showed on the handsome, strong features that rarely showed uncalculated reaction.

He gave her a repressing look. "I believe that should come after you have agreed to marry me."

"You don't think it might help me agree?" Or not. If they had no chemistry.

Which on her side she had no doubts of, but her doubts in his genuine attraction for her were growing with each date that ended without so much as a kiss on the cheek.

"I will not allow sex to influence my choices and would prefer you weren't under the influence of sexual need when you make yours."

"You do expect to have sex though? After we are married?" He didn't really anticipate using IVF to get her pregnant, did he?

She didn't realize she'd asked that last out loud until the look of shocked horror on his features told her she had.

"Yes, we will have sex. There will be no test-tube babies for us."

"Okay. Good."

"Your lifestyle to this point has not indicated a desire for sexual intimacy."

"I've already explained that to you." She made no effort to prevaricate.

For whatever reason, she didn't want Nikolai to believe she'd ever gone to bed with another man while she would have been perfectly happy for Konstantin to make that assumption.

"You have already told me you are attracted to me. Are you saying that is not true?" he asked her, like a man trying to figure out a very difficult puzzle.

It was all she could do not to give in to sarcasm. He could not be that dense. "It's not my attraction to you that I'm doubting."

"But I told you I wanted you," he said like that should be it.

The final word on the subject.

"I think with some things, actions speak with more assurance than words."

"We are not having sex before our wedding night."

He laid down the law like the King he was. "Our first child will be conceived within the bounds of marriage. As heir to my throne it would be grossly unfair for us to risk anything else."

"There are such things as birth control."

"We can wait."

She sat back into the corner of her seat, her arms crossed over her chest, feeling very put out and knowing he would not understand why *at all*. "Of course we can. Far be it from the King of Mirrus to act with spontaneity."

"I had my fill of spontaneity a long time ago." His expression said his memories in that direction were not good ones.

When he'd been married? Before that? After? She wanted to ask. So badly but knew she wouldn't.

Because as much as he'd guessed about her life as a child, she had no plans to ever share the memories that still haunted her nightmares.

With an imprecation, he grabbed his phone and sent a text, then crossed the limousine to join her on the leather upholstery on her side.

She stared up at him. "What's going on?"

"I'm letting my past dictate my present and that's as stupid as reliving it."

"You're not making any sense."

But the expression in his eyes was saying plenty. His gray eyes were molten with desire, his body rigid with self-restraint. And that's when she knew he wanted her too.

"You *want* to kiss me," she said wonderingly.

"Yes," he ground out.

"So, do it!" Why did men always make things so complicated?

She gasped in shock when he took her up on her offer. Nikolai's tongue was right there sliding between her parted lips. This was no polite peck of lips.

Nikolai took possession of her mouth with passionate domination and Nataliya fell into the kiss with every bit of desire coursing through her virginal body.

He pulled her close, one hand cupping her breast through the lace of her gown and she moaned. She'd never been touched like this. She'd never even been kissed with tongue.

And she liked it all. Every new sensation building something inside her so that unfamiliar tension coiled within her.

She put her hands on his chest, squeezing his pecs, then feeling down his stomach, wishing his shirt were not in the way.

He made a sexy growling sound deep in his chest and yanked her into his lap, deepening the kiss. Everything went hazy, passion burning all rational thought from Nataliya's brain as the kiss went on and on and on.

He carefully peeled the fabric away from her body, slid his hand into the bodice of her dress and cupped her breast, pinching her aching nipple between her thumb and forefinger.

She let out a little cry against his lips, overwhelmed by the amazing sensation, and the pleasure in her core spiraled tighter.

He rolled her nipple back and forth, sending pleasure

zinging directly from there to between her legs and unfamiliar feelings built inside her until she felt like she
would scream with them.

It was too much and not enough and she did not know
how to ask for what she needed. But then he pulled her
closer and she felt his hardness against her hip, through
their clothes, and something about that intimacy just
sent her pleasure skyrocketing. The most amazing sensations washed over her until her body went rigid with
her climax.

She ripped her lips from his to let the pleasure out
in a scream and he kissed down her neck and back up
to her mouth.

"So perfect, so passionate," he said in a tone that only
added to the pleasure floating over her.

She collapsed against him, awash with sensation but
so lethargic she could not have moved for anything.

"Sexually compatible." This time his tone was pure
smug arrogance.

And even that didn't turn her off.

"Last word again?"

"I deserve it, don't you think?"

"Maybe this time."

He rapped his knuckles on the window and that must
have been some kind of signal because minutes later,
the limousine slid to a stop.

The door did not open however and she was grateful.
He helped her get herself back together and off his lap.

"I will see you tomorrow," he reminded her.

They had plans to go on a tour of Central Park, because she'd said she wanted to. Later, they were going to have dinner together again.

Another perfect date.

Maybe it would end with another perfect kiss.

CHAPTER FIVE

KISSING NATALIYA HAD BEEN a good decision.

No way was she still worried that he did not desire her. As if.

If anything, his sexual feelings for her were so strong, he had almost dismissed his idea of fulfilling the contract in his brother's stead out of hand. Nikolai refused to be at the mercy of his libido. Again.

Only he'd realized that wanting her was not a bad thing. Having her would be a better thing. All he had to do was keep his emotional distance and never allow her to use his desire for her to control him.

Knowing that she wanted him, had always wanted him, even when she'd tried her best to hide it? That gave him the certainty that she would not withhold herself from him as Tiana had done. Would not use his desire as a weapon against him.

Nataliya was too honest and forthright to play those kinds of games, regardless.

He ignored the small voice telling him that all women were capable. He would not put himself in a position for sex to become a bargaining chip.

Never again.

But that did not mean he could not allay her fears on that score.

Nikolai was proud of both his superior decision making skills in sharing that intimacy with her. When she had climaxed in his arms, he'd wanted to shout in triumph. Nataliya had proven she could not withhold her reactions from him and that was something he needed to know after the pain of his first marriage, where sex had been a bargaining chip, a battleground, but never just pleasure.

And though her response to him had shot his libido into the stratosphere, he'd maintained the control he'd fought to hone.

He'd wanted to take her right there in the limousine, but he hadn't even undressed her. Nataliya's uninhibited passionate response had been deliciously surprising and nearly obliterating to his self-control.

But he *had* controlled himself and that was what mattered.

As he'd told Nataliya, his heir would not be conceived outside the legal bonds of matrimony.

A marriage he had no doubts *would* take place regardless of her posturing.

So, she wanted a proposal. He was a king, but he was also a man with superior intellect. He would give her the proposal of her dreams and she would finally agree verbally to what they both knew was a foregone conclusion.

Their marriage.

Nataliya was relieved that Jenna and her boyfriend were not back yet when she entered the hotel suite.

She needed some time. To parse what that kiss meant.

No way could she legitimately wonder if he wanted her. He'd been hard and she'd felt it. The fact he hadn't taken it farther than a kiss was a tick in the plus column. Nikolai could and would control his own sexual desires when necessary.

That boded well for the concept of fidelity.

Even so, she needed time to deal with the emotional aftermath of her first orgasm with another person and how vulnerable it made her feel.

Because as much as she respected that he hadn't pushed for more, the fact she was the only one who had come was a little disconcerting. She'd never seen herself as very sexual. Yes, she'd always wanted him, but in a vague, undefined way.

She'd experimented with toys, but her pleasure had taken longer to achieve and not been as devastating.

Far from having the slow fuse she'd always thought, with him, it was short and explosive.

Oh, man. So explosive.

It was time to do some research.

Research she should have done weeks ago, but she'd been putting off.

She didn't want to do a deep dive into Nikolai's life, but she wasn't marrying a man who had a long-term mistress like her uncle or a string of them like his own brother and her father.

She needed to know just how he lived his life now and if he was currently involved with another woman.

You could just ask, her conscience reminded her.

But Nataliya needed cold hard facts and as much as she knew Nikolai expected every word he uttered to be taken as gospel, her past made that kind of blind trust impossible.

She ordered a pot of coffee and pulled out the laptop that beat her desktop for speed and memory. It was a pretty cool betrothal gift. Sort of fitting she was using it to check out how smart betrothal to the King would be then.

Several hours later, Nataliya had some answers. And they were all good ones.

She'd hacked into his financial records, run his name and face through her personalized media and social media search engine. She'd checked out every single instance of travel for him in the past year, every expenditure in and out of country and done a less thorough but adequate search for the years since his wife's death.

Everything had come back empty. No apartments paid for by him but occupied by a woman. He'd had companions at some of the more prominent social functions, but he'd usually brought a cousin who was now married to one of his top aides. Nothing that would indicate he had liaisons, mistresses or even the occasional lover since his Queen's passing.

In short, on paper anyway, he was her dream guy.

For a woman, who had never thought to marry for love, that was a pretty big deal.

Nataliya woke after about four hours' sleep, still tired but feeling more solid about this royal courtship she was experiencing. She'd known Nikolai was not a carbon copy of his brother, but she'd needed to be sure.

About the fidelity thing. About the fact that there

were no other personal contenders for the position of his Princess.

There would always be plenty of women with the right breeding and the desire for the role, but he had not been courting any of them.

Which meant what?

That he *wanted* her in that role? That the timing had been right, and he'd decided to remarry just when his brother was deciding to renege on the contract?

She couldn't dismiss the honor thing, because she'd come to accept that for Nikolai, maintaining family honor and fulfilling his house's terms in the contract were very important to him. Like obsession-level importance.

Whether he'd been raised with an overweening sense of integrity, or it was something innate in Nikolai. Either way, she no longer disregarded it as a very real motivation for him.

And that gave her hope for their future if they were to have one. A man that focused on maintaining family and personal integrity would not look at his marriage vows as multiple-choice options.

And he wanted her. He'd proven that.

Regardless of what others in her position might think, that mattered. As his Princess, Nataliya would lose all the trappings of a *normal* life she'd worked so hard to attain, but she would insist on having a stable and normal marriage, or as normal as possible married to a king who was also a billionaire business mogul.

That meant sharing a bed and a life. She was not Queen Oxana, and Nataliya would not spend her life finding satisfaction in her duty and her position.

There had to be more.

She'd seen that more in Maks's and Demyan's marriages, knew that even if her husband did not love her, he could give Nataliya more than what she'd seen between her aunt and uncle or her own parents, much less the other royals of that generation in Volyarus.

She would have more, or she would not marry.

No matter what she'd signed when she was eighteen.

Later, Nataliya was not at all surprised that they were going to have a horse-drawn carriage for their tour of Central Park.

Nikolai had a canny knack for knowing what she might enjoy most.

She was surprised, however, that the carriage looked so elegant and that it was drawn by two perfectly matched horses of the kind of quality she recognized as beyond the means of the average tourist company.

"Are these your horses?" she asked him in shock.

"They are now." He flashed her a slashing, arrogant smile. "I bought them from stables with an excellent reputation in Upstate New York."

"And the carriage?"

"Purchased for this occasion."

"You don't think that's a little over the top?"

"I am a king, Nataliya. I do not ride in conveyances that cater to the masses."

But to *buy* a carriage? "You sound really snobby right now."

"Not simply intelligent about my own safety?"

He was talking about assassination attempts. In his father's lifetime, the former King had survived one and she had no idea if Nikolai had ever been the target of such an attempt. She had no doubt that if he had, he would have kept it very quiet.

"I stand corrected," she acknowledged. "But I still think you have no clue how the average person lives."

"And you do." He said it with satisfaction.

Nataliya gave him a surprised look. "You like that?"

"Very much. Mirrusians live all over the globe in all walks of life. The royal family should understand them if we are expected to serve their needs."

"That's a very progressive view."

"I am a progressive man."

A man who was getting married based on a contract his father had signed? She did not think so. "Maybe in some things."

"I am no throwback."

"No, I'd say you are the inevitable product of growing up royal in the twenty-first century in a country that is still a full monarchy."

"Volyarus is also a monarchy."

"I am aware." She settled back into the comfortable leather squabs of the carriage. "What happens to this carriage after today?"

"It will be sold and the proceeds donated to the charity we've been supporting with our courtship."

"Konstantin didn't like my online auction."

"You hit at his pride."

"It was intentional," she admitted. "But you provide gifts *for* the auction."

"It is a worthy cause." He took her hand, in an unexpected public display of affection that should be entirely innocent.

Only she felt that touch go right through her and had to take a deep breath and let it out slowly not to give herself away.

His knowing look said she hadn't been all that successful. "So, going back to our earlier words, are you a proponent of constitutional monarchy?" he asked, but didn't sound worried or even shocked by the idea she might be.

"Power should always be checked."

"And those checks, do they always work?" He brushed his thumb over her palm, sending electric sparks along that nerve-rich center and up her arm.

She curled her fingers around his thumb to stop him so she could think clearly enough to focus on answering him. "No, but having them gives the people that power is supposed to protect more of a chance of actually enjoying that protection."

"Does your uncle know you have these prorepublic leanings?" Amusement laced Nikolai's tone.

"Technically, he is my second cousin."

"But he sees himself in a closer role. You call him uncle."

"Not anymore, I don't." It had taken her long enough, but she'd come to realize that family was more than a word. It was a relationship, and her "uncle" had removed himself from their relationship a long time ago.

Now that seemed to startle Nikolai, when her beliefs that *his* power should be checked by a parliament didn't. "Why not?"

"Fifteen years ago, he sacrificed me and my mother to protect his good name when the whole time he has

been the biggest risk to scandal in the royal family."
Mama had always known too.

Nataliya had only learned of her King's infidelity as
an adult and quite by accident, but then she'd spoken to
her mother about it, hurt and angered by the monarch's
hypocrisy. She'd learned then that Mama had known
since the beginning.

It had sparked one of their rare arguments.

"Because of his long-term mistress."

"Exactly." The woman he'd refused to marry because
of her divorce but had never been willing to give up.
"You know about their long-term affair. She's not the
secret he believes she is. If the media starts digging,
they won't have to go very deep to reach a royal scandal of epic proportions."

"You do not think King Fedir has things in place to
protect the monarchy in such an event?"

"He may think he does, but his relationship is too
long-standing for him to deny it with any chance at
being believed. Too many people know about it. Too
many bills have been paid for her through the palace
accounts."

"I'm sure King Fedir has taken precautions so that
those bills cannot be traced back to him."

"I traced them. And as we both saw at the hackathon, I'm good, but I'm by no means the only good
hacker out there."

"You hacked into your uncle's financial records?"

"I hacked into the palace financial records."

"You didn't know about the mistress," he said in
wonder.

"Before we left Volyarus, no I did not. In fact, I did not discover her existence until a few years ago."

"And realizing he maintained that relationship put a different complexion on his actions with you and your mother fifteen years ago."

"Yes. I realized that he expects everyone but himself to sacrifice for the sake of *his* throne."

"Isn't that a bit harsh? He has a whole country's well-being he must take into account."

"Not if it means giving up the woman he loves, but not enough to marry. If you can call the sort of selfishness that drives him love at all."

"You judge him harshly."

"I paid a high price for his pride, but Mama, who had already paid a terrible price for being married to my father, was forced to give up even more." And Nataliya wasn't sure she would ever forgive her King for making her mother pay that price.

"The Countess seems to have built a good life for herself in her exile."

"Mama has, but she should not have had to learn to live without her family and friends. It wasn't fair."

"Do you feel that way about the contract? That it is not fair?"

Nataliya thought about that for a minute, never having put the contract in those terms.

"I think me being pressured to sign it and accept the terms when I was eighteen was not fair. I would fight tooth and nail to stop my own child from doing the same."

He nodded but said nothing. Still waiting it seemed for her to answer the core of his question.

Did she think it fair that she was contracted to marry him?

Instead of answering that, she offered some truth of her own. "I did a deep dive into your life last night."

"I thought you looked tired." He took both her hands in his and smiled down at her, obviously not worried about her investigation. "Did you get any sleep?"

"A few hours." She licked her lips, her gaze caught on his mouth, wanting to taste.

His gray gaze darkened with desire. "A nap might be in order this afternoon."

Was he offering to take it with her? She shook her head. No, of course not.

"Is that all you're going to say?" Nataliya asked, stunned he wasn't offended.

"What do you want me to say? I cannot claim I did not expect you to use your skills to discover if I have any skeletons in my closet. Your main concern about marrying Konstantin was his tendency to have uncommitted sex with women."

"He wasn't in a relationship, not like my father."

"But it still gave you pause."

"You know it did."

"You would not have found anything similar in my background."

"Not even a discreet long-term mistress."

"I am not King Fedir either."

"No. You are kind of an anomaly among powerful men. I'd wonder if you had a repressed libido, but I felt the evidence of your arousal in the car last night."

Far from being insulted by her remark, he laughed.

"I can assure you, my libido is everything you will want it to be."

"I don't doubt it." She looked to their tour guide-slash-carriage driver and only now realized he had earbuds in.

She probably should have noticed he wasn't giving a running commentary, but Nataliya had been so caught up in Nikolai, for once in her adult life, she hadn't paid the utmost attention to the situation around her.

His smile said he knew. "Just noticed he's in hear-no-evil, or rather *private discussion* mode?"

"Yes."

"That's not like you."

"I thought we were doing a tour."

"The commentary will start when I give him a signal."

"Your guards are in the pedicabs ahead of and behind us, aren't they?" She'd just noticed that too.

"They wanted to be riding their own horses, but you would not believe the regulations governing any and all activity in Central Park."

"Even a king has to submit to red tape."

He nodded, his expression rueful. "If I'd had more time…"

He'd had time enough to buy gorgeous matching horses and a carriage.

He did some more of that thumb brushing, this time on both of her palms and she shivered.

"You wouldn't have been sure of me, if I hadn't kissed you last night." He sounded very pleased with himself.

"Maybe. I'm not sure," she admitted. "I kind of see

you as this larger than life man. Yes, you are a king, but you're not a despot."

"You don't think so?" he asked, like her opinion actually mattered.

"You're the kind of king that makes me not worry about you not having a parliament, unless I'm worried about you taking too much on and not having anyone else to help carry the burden." Why was she being *so* honest? She'd never have been this open with anyone else.

Nikolai's expression could be seen as nothing less than satisfaction. "King Fedir?"

"Would benefit a lot by having some checks of power in his life."

"So, you think I am a good king?"

"Yes."

"And a good man?" he asked.

"Yes." She'd always thought so, but she'd had to be sure.

"You have no questions about things you may have discovered last night?"

"I didn't discover anything. That's the point, isn't it? Were there things to discover?"

"About me? No."

"Then about who?"

"Does it matter?"

If his father, or brother, or someone else had done something she might have questions about? "No. I don't think it does, but you would tell me, wouldn't you, if there was something that would affect me?"

"Yes." Nikolai looked so stern when he said that, but not shifty.

So, she believed.

"I think if I were a different woman, raised in a different way, I might think the contract was unfair," she said, finally answering his initial question. "If *you* were a different man, you wouldn't feel the need to fulfill its terms on behalf of your house."

"Perhaps."

"But I am who I am. And honestly, I wasn't raised to believe in fairy tales and happy endings. I don't remember Mama ever suggesting she hoped I found true love." More like Solomia had hoped her daughter would not end up married to a man who would physically hurt her.

But even with that hope, Mama had still encouraged her daughter to sign that contract ten years ago, with no idea about what kind of man Konstantin was.

"I don't think the contract itself is unfair." Nataliya acknowledged as much to herself as to him. "I *did* sign it. I did agree to the terms. I never expected to marry a man I loved, but I won't marry a man I cannot trust."

"My brother is trustworthy."

"Maybe, but his double standard about dating and sex make it hard for me to see him that way." She didn't want to talk about his brother. "Regardless, if we marry and are blessed with children, then believe their well-being will be more important to me than that of Mirrus."

"But that is not how a royal thinks."

"Then I guess you'd better make sure I never have to choose between duty and my children."

"That's a heavy promise you want me to make."

"No. My promise to you is that if you don't succeed

at that, I will not be browbeaten into doing something that could hurt those I love. Period."

"That is the perspective of the common man."

"A perspective you said the royal family needs."

"Yes."

"So, that implies you are going to take my opinions into consideration when making decisions for Mirrus."

"It does, yes."

"But you hardly know me."

"You are not the only hacker available to dive deep into someone's life."

"Plus your family has had me under surveillance for ten years." Someone paying attention could know a great deal about her.

"That is true."

"You've read the reports?" she couldn't help asking.

"All of them."

All of them? "That's a lot of reading."

"Deciding to enforce the contract and fulfill its terms was not a spur-of-the-moment decision. I do not make those." He said the last like his own warning.

"I believe it." Though at first that was exactly what she'd thought he'd done. "You came to Volyarus intending to put yourself forward as the Prince of your house referred to in the contract."

"I did."

"Did Konstantin know?"

"No. It is not my habit to take others into my confidence."

"I think I'll expect you to take me into your confidence, if I marry you."

"We are separate people. Our duties will live in harmony but not always overlap."

"Are you trying to warn me that I won't see much of you if I marry you?" That might actually turn out to be the deal breaker nothing else had.

His jaw went taut. "That will be up to you."

"What do you mean?" she asked, her brows drawn together in confusion.

"Though I travel some for diplomatic reasons, all business travel is Konstantin's purview. I spend most of my time in Mirrus."

"Wouldn't your wife do the same?"

"Tiana did not. She found life in Mirrus stifling and preferred traveling with friends in warmer climates."

That made no sense. No more sense that he would tolerate it. "But she was the Queen. Surely her duties precluded long vacations in Jamaica."

"Monaco was her favorite haunt, but as to her duties, she found those stifling, as well."

Nataliya didn't know what he thought about that. His expression revealed nothing.

"I am used to working long hours," she offered.

"Will you expect to continue with a career after marriage?" Something about that question made him so tense, she couldn't miss it, despite how he was so careful to maintain an expressionless mask.

"If I were to marry a king, I think the job of being his Princess would keep me sufficiently busy."

"Not all women would agree."

"Really? I can't imagine a single woman of my acquaintance who would attempt to maintain a full-time career as well as the full-time job of Princess."

"So you do see it as a job."

"Being a wife is a role, but being a princess? That's definitely a job."

"I'm very glad to hear you say that."

What else didn't she know about his marriage to Tiana? Nataliya had not known that Tiana spent so much time away from Mirrus, but she'd been careful in her research to respect Nikolai's personal privacy. Other than confirming that Tiana had not had a bunch of visits from the Palace Physician for unexplained injuries, Nataliya had purposefully not looked too deeply into his marriage.

Just because she *could* find out just about anything about a person's life, didn't mean she *would* do that. It was a matter of her own personal integrity.

They spent the rest of their tour talking about their families, getting to know each other on a level that no amount of reading investigative reports could achieve. Nikolai never did indicate their tour guide start his commentary.

And she didn't mind at all.

She wasn't surprised she enjoyed the King's company.

Nataliya always had.

He was the guy she'd had her first crush on and being older and wiser only made those feelings seem deeper. But she didn't love him.

Would not let herself.

She felt something for him though, that would make refusing marriage to him impossible.

Not that she was sharing that revelation with the arrogant King.

CHAPTER SIX

NATALIYA DID END UP taking a long nap that afternoon because their dinner reservations weren't until eight.

Nataliya expected to be taken to an exclusive five-star restaurant with a month-long waiting list for dinner.

Because so far Nikolai had pulled out all the stops for this courtship.

So, she was a little surprised to find herself at Central Park for the second time that day. An eight-person security team surrounded them as they exited the limousine.

"What are we doing back here?"

"Having dinner."

"I thought we had reservations."

"I said dinner was at eight. And it will be." He sounded so complacent, almost smug, like he knew what he'd planned was going to please her.

She couldn't help wanting to push his buttons a little. Laughing, she said, "I'm not exactly dressed for a picnic with hot dogs from a local vendor," she teased.

The look of horror on his face was worth the tease. "Trust me—that is not what we are having for dinner."

"You're such a snob." She found herself reaching for

his hand and having to pull hers back before the telling movement gave her away.

He made it so easy to forget they weren't really dating. That this courtship was the result of a contract signed a long time ago.

"I am a king. I would and have eaten grubs in order not to offend my hosts in both Africa and Australia, but if the choice of venue is up to me? We are never eating from a food truck." He spoke with the conviction he usually reserved for matters of real import.

It made her smile. "I'm not sure hot dog carts are considered food trucks, but I get your point. Thousands of foodies would tell you that you don't know what you are missing though."

"I will live with the loss," he said dryly.

She shook her head, her smile undimmed. "You just watch. One day I'll convince you."

"Watch yourself, *kiska*. You are sounding dangerously like you are considering a future with me."

"Perhaps you should be the one watching out. Maybe I am," she admitted, some things having solidified inside her while she'd slept and rejuvenated that afternoon.

"I am very glad to hear that." He was the one who reached for her hand, bringing it to his mouth to kiss the inside of her palm.

She gasped, that small salute sending tingles of pleasure right to the core of her. It was not a carnal act, but her body's reaction was as basic as it got. Nataliya craved Nikolai like she'd never desired another man, and the more time they spent together the stronger that craving got.

It scared her and excited her at the same time.

Knowing that she was developing a need for him that only he would ever be able to fill frightened her, but the knowledge he wanted to marry her mitigated that fear.

If he were a man like her father, she'd run fast and far from both her feelings and him, but Nikolai would never betray her as the Count had betrayed Nataliya's mother over and over again.

They came into a clearing and unexpected tears pricked her eyes at what she saw.

It was so over-the-top, but even at first glance the amount of thought that went into setting it up was obvious.

Standing lanterns surrounded a table set with the official linens she'd only seen in the Mirrus palace. Eggshell white, they were embroidered in gold and navy blue with the coat of arms for the House of Merikov. Fine white bone china with the same design sat atop gold chargers she had no doubt were pure precious metal and the crystal on the table sparkled elegantly.

The eight-person security detail, rather than his usual four, suddenly made sense. The table settings alone were worth thousands, if not tens of thousands and the centerpiece looked like a vase Oxana had in her sitting room. Mama had told her as a child not to touch it because it was priceless.

When royalty used that term, they meant it.

But beyond the opulence of the setting was how much care had been taken to bring a taste of Mirrus to New York. A small, ornate, gold-leafed trinket box sat next to one of the place settings.

It didn't take a computer genius to know what was

in that box. The official betrothal ring of the House of Merikov.

"It's beautiful," Nataliya said in a hushed voice, that trinket box taking her breath away.

Nikolai led her to the table, relinquishing her hand to pull Nataliya's chair out himself. "I have pleased you. I am glad."

"You've been pleasing me this whole courtship, and you know it." She made the mistake of looking up and found herself frozen by the molten depths of his gaze.

"I have tried."

Oh, man. She needed to get a hold of herself. Forcing herself to look away, she settled into her chair. "Enough with the false humility, Nikolai," she mocked, though she felt like doing anything but mocking. "You are a king. You do not consider failure as an option."

That ornate trinket box to the left of her plate affirmed that truth as much as it stole the very breath from her body.

He moved around the table and took his own seat, his attention fixed firmly on her. "And yet, to succeed, ultimately I need your cooperation."

"It's nice to hear you finally admit that."

His left brow rose in sardonic question. "I have never denied that your agreement is necessary."

"But you *have* acted like you assume you already had it." And why it should strike her that that kind of arrogance could be sexy, she did not know.

"You signed the contract, but only you can decide if you are going to fulfill its terms." He flicked his hand to signal someone.

A waiter came out of the darkness around them to

shake out Nataliya's napkin and lay it smoothly across her lap before doing the same for Nikolai. Moments later, water and wine were poured in their crystal goblets and a starter of fresh prawns was served over a bed of arugula.

She savored a prawn before smiling at him, because she wanted to. "My favorite."

"I know."

"How?" she asked curiously, pretty sure she hadn't mentioned this weakness to him.

"A man reading your comings, goings and habits for the past ten years can learn a great deal if he wants to." And would be a fool not to, his tone implied.

After all the deep dives into someone else's life she'd done for Demyan, as well as the one she'd done on Nikolai, it felt strange to know that a *king* had spent so much time not only reading up on her but interpreting the very mundane details recorded by those who had watched *her* over the past decade. "And you wanted to?"

"Can you doubt it?"

"It just seems like overkill for you to pay such close attention."

"Does it? Didn't you do the same?"

"Not really, no. I only looked at certain areas of your life for the past couple of years." She'd been interested in patterns that would reveal behaviors she could not live with.

Nataliya had been content to learn his likes, dislikes and views through the more regular method of simply getting to know him.

"Believe me, after my first marriage, I had no desire to be surprised by any aspect of your life or nature."

He made it sound like his first marriage had offered up some unpleasant surprises.

Remembering the way he'd been with his Queen, Nataliya found that difficult to believe.

But then, who looking at her family would ever have guessed her father was the violent man he had been with her and Mama?

"Doesn't that take some of the mystique out of it?" As she asked the question, Nataliya realized how foolish it was.

That kind of mystique belonged in romance, but their relationship was not based on anything so emotive.

His look said he was surprised by the question. "I do not think a marriage for a sovereign needs to have mystique."

"I would say you do not have a romantic bone in your body," she teased, covering her own embarrassment at the knowledge that very thing wasn't what they were about. "But this whole scenario says otherwise."

Which was no less than the truth, so maybe, he could take a little bit of the blame for how hard she found it to remember this courtship wasn't about romance.

"You deserve to be treated as the special woman you are, but that does not make me romantic," he said decisively.

Warmth unfurled inside her at his words, despite how surprised she was by his claim.

"You don't consider yourself romantic?" she asked, startled.

The man had been nothing but romantic in his courtship of her, despite the fact it was based on all sorts of things *besides* romance.

"Romance is based on illusion and I have no illusions left."

Okay. No question. His marriage had *not* been the perfect union she had always assumed, unless he'd had a relationship she didn't know about since Tiana's death.

"You sound so cynical, but that is not how you treat me." And she was glad.

"There is nothing about you which to be cynical about," he said with some satisfaction.

"I'm not perfect." Not even a paragon. She was after all the woman who had embarked on the first dates article in order to get Konstantin to back out of the contract when her King refused to renegotiate its terms to leave her out of it.

"No, but your integrity is bone-deep and your understanding of duty uncommon in the current age."

She found it interesting he believed so strongly in her honesty, knowing how she'd sought to manipulate his brother. But then she hadn't done anything *wrong* in her efforts to get out of the contract. Maybe more than anything, that revealed how much this King did not believe in the double standard of fidelity so many men in positions of power seemed hampered by.

Nevertheless, she reminded him, "We've had this discussion."

"Yes. You have promised that if it came between our children's happiness and duty, you would choose their happiness. That is not a deterrent to me."

"Apparently it's not." But she didn't understand how it wasn't. Did he think she'd give in when it came down to it?

He would learn differently if the situation ever arose.

"We share the knowledge that more than our own happiness rests on our shoulders, but the well-being of an entire country. That does not mean we will both not make every effort to see our children happy that we can."

That was good to hear, but too practically put to justify the squishy warmth inside her right now.

Doing her best to ignore those feelings, she acknowledged, "I was raised to understand my place in the world and that it was not the same place as Jenna's, or the other *normal* people like her."

Nataliya had done her best to have a normal life, but she belonged to the royal family of Volyarus and always would do.

He nodded. "Jenna, while a good friend, does not have the welfare of a country to consider when she decides how she spends her time."

"You're saying I do." Despite her ever-present knowledge of her place in the world, Nataliya had never really thought that she took that into account in *everything* she did, but she wasn't sure she could deny it either.

"You always have."

When she'd been little, Nataliya had known she could not talk about what happened in her home, not only because of the shame she and her mom felt, but because *a lady did not tell tales*. And she had known she was Lady Nataliya since she knew her own name.

As she'd grown older, that knowledge of who she was *had* continued to influence her. When she'd been tempted to test her hacking skills at the university in ways others did, she'd stopped herself, knowing if she got caught it could bring embarrassment to the royal family.

One of the reasons she was so good was that she'd had to be positive she could not be traced or trapped when she tried a hack. Her absolute need not to be caught had made her better.

Nataliya hadn't been born a princess, but she had been born into the royal family.

Because her father had been such an embarrassment to the throne, she and Mama had been forced to make choices for the good of Volyarus even other nobility of their country would not be required to make.

While those choices had hurt, Nataliya had never denied they were necessary.

The way the exile had been handled by King and Queen? That had not been okay.

The way she and Mama had been made into pariahs right along with her father? That had not been okay.

The fact that her mother's exile had never been lifted? That had not been okay either.

But Nataliya did not resent her place in the world or what it required of her to fill it.

"If it had been up to you, would you have left my mother living in exile for all these years?" she asked him as their soup course was laid.

"You mean, if I had been in your uncle's position? I should hope that I would show more concern for one of my subjects, much less a woman as close to me as a sister. It is true that in life we are sometimes called to pay the price for another's sin, but it is not my habit to dismiss that cost to others."

"Have you ever been faced with a similar situation?"

"Yes, I have." But he did not elaborate and then Niko-lai frowned. "However, in a very real way, it was up to me. I did not pressure my brother into fulfilling the terms of the contract."

"Why not?"

"I was allowed to choose my wife."

"And you felt guilty that he had not."

"Yes." He paused, considered, like he was decid-ing how much he wanted to say. "That was part of it certainly."

"What was the other part?"

He approved the wine for the soup course and then met her gaze, his mysterious and dark. "When you were a teenager, you used to watch me like I was a football star."

"You knew about my crush?" She should have been embarrassed, but somehow she wasn't.

She wasn't ashamed of the feelings she'd once had for him, even if she never wanted to be that emotion-ally vulnerable again.

That crush had turned into unrequited love that she had not managed to stifle despite her best efforts until he'd lost his wife and his grief acted as a barrier to her heart she'd never been able to erect on her own.

"I did and I felt it was unfair on you both to press forward a marriage that would cause you both discom-fort if not pain under those circumstances."

She'd never thought he'd noticed her obsession with him. Nataliya gave Nikolai a self-deprecating smile. "I thought I was so good at hiding it."

"Who of us as teenagers is that good at hiding any-thing?" he asked with some amusement.

"I'm pretty sure that even as a teenager, you were an expert at hiding any feelings you did not want to share."

"I had posters of…" He named a popular American film star. "All over my side of the room at boarding school."

"But she would have been old enough to be your mother!" Nataliya exclaimed, laughing.

"I thought she was everything sexy."

"And now?" Nataliya asked, wondering if he had another secret celebrity crush.

Nikolai gave her a sultry look. "My tastes have refined. I'm turned on by sexy computer hackers who forget dates."

"I didn't forget—I was late."

"Because you forgot."

How did a woman forget a date with a king? She didn't, but the first week of his courtship, Nataliya had gotten caught up in her work to the extent that Jenna's frantic phone call wondering where she was had been necessary.

"You weren't angry you had to wait."

"Naturally not. I find it admirable that you take your work so seriously."

"The duty thing again?" She sighed and knew she owed him the truth. "It's not about focusing so seriously on my job—it's that I really get lost in it and have no awareness of time passing or even people coming in and out of the room with me."

"I find that charming." His heated look said he found it something else too. Hot.

How? She didn't know, but she was glad. "Here's

hoping that doesn't change because I'm unlikely to. It's a personality trait."

"You're very blunt."

Her mouth twisted in consternation. "Not a great trait for a diplomat, I know."

"For a princess who is a diplomat by role rather than career, I do not agree. I believe that your ability to be forthright will be a benefit to our House."

She laughed. Couldn't help doing so. "You're the only one who has ever considered that flaw a strength." Even her beloved mother found Nataliya's blunt manner something to censure.

"Honesty is not a flaw."

"Even when I say truths I shouldn't?"

"I have never heard you say anything you shouldn't," he claimed.

"Um, are you practicing selective memory, or lying?" she asked.

"Neither."

"But I offended your father and your brother during that little tribunal at the Volyarussian palace."

"And their attitude to you offended me."

"It did?" She thought about how Nikolai had responded in that confrontation. "It did."

"Yes. Nothing you said that day should not have been said," he repeated with an approving smile. "So, you too saw it as a tribunal?"

"What else? My so-called *uncle* and your father, not to mention your brother, were determined to put me on trial."

"And instead they found themselves on the wrong

side of having to defend their own actions and attitudes."

Looking back, she realized that was true. No one had expected her to take them to task, but she had. And Nikolai, without condemning his own brother, had backed her up.

So had Oxana and Mama, in their own ways.

They ate in companionable silence for a few minutes before she said, "I've been thinking about what I would like to do careerwise if I were to become The Princess of Mirrus."

Subtle tension filled his body, like he had gone on alert. "Yes?"

"I would like to continue what I do for Demyan…" she trailed off when that subtle tension went overt.

His jaw went hard, his body going ramrod straight, but all he said was, "Yes?"

"I like what I do, but I wasn't sure there was a place for me at Mirrus Global."

The tension drained out of Nikolai and his smile was blinding. "You want to use your powers for my company rather than Yurkovich-Tanner?" His delight at the idea was unmistakable.

She grinned. "Yes, but only part-time."

"Because you understand that to be my Princess is in itself a job that requires time and attention? I could not have chosen a better lady to stand at my side if I had searched the world over."

The compliment was over-the-top, but she got the distinct impression he meant every word and that did things to her heart she didn't want to examine too closely. "You really are something special, you know that?"

"Because I like the idea of headhunting my own wife from my rival?" he asked, in full arrogant-guy mode.

She rolled her eyes at him. "Yurkovich-Tanner is not your rival. You are business partners."

"But I have been jealous of Demyan's hacker for years."

"You didn't know it was me." She didn't make it a question.

Nataliya and Demyan had done an excellent job of hiding her true role at Yurkovich-Tanner since she'd been hired on and he discovered her abilities as a hacker.

She was the one who had discovered the Crown Princess's pregnancy after Gillian and Maks broke up. Demyan had used Nataliya on the most delicate matters. Only now did she realize that was because he had always seen her as family, and he trusted her implicitly.

"I did not." Nikolai winked. "Once we found out at the *tribunal* I was worried you would want to continue working for your cousin."

That's why Nikolai had gone all tense just now? He'd been thinking about it even then?

"When I marry, my loyalty will belong first and foremost to my husband." She was still talking in couched terms, but it needed to be said.

"That is a great boon coming from a woman with such a formidable sense of loyalty."

She shrugged, a little embarrassed. "You're always so complimentary."

"I think very highly of you. I would have thought you would have realized that by now."

Coming from the man she admired above all others, that was kind of an amazing thing to hear. More than amazing, it touched Nataliya's heart in that uncomfortable way all over again and even filled it.

Everything around her went into sharp focus as something she had simply not allowed herself to see became glaringly obvious. This one man touched her emotions in a way no one else did, and with a simple compliment, because he lived in her heart.

She still loved him.

She'd never stopped, though she'd done a good job of pretending to herself for the sake of her own sense of honor.

She'd felt bad for loving a married man, and like a monster when he'd lost the wife *he'd* loved. Nataliya had also realized it was not fair to love one brother and marry another.

So, she'd convinced herself that her *crush* was over, that her feelings for Nikolai were nothing more than teenage hormones.

But this feeling inside her was so big, she could barely contain it. She adored the man who had always been her hero.

At first, she'd just had an almighty crush on the man, but she'd learned to respect so much about him from early on. Yes, he'd taken over as King for the sake of his father's health, but Nikolai had done so with a fully developed agenda that put the people of Mirrus first. He was a staunch conservationist and environmentalist which wasn't easy to manage with the economic needs of his country, but he did it.

He was respectful to others, didn't lose his temper

or throw around his weight just because he could and he was loyal to his family. Loyal like her own uncle only pretended to be.

Had *he* been the reason she'd been so determined to end that contract? Had her subconscious finally realized that she simply could *not* marry his brother?

She couldn't be sure that it played no part and she wasn't sure how that made her feel.

Because her integrity was important to her.

"I think I still have a crush on you," she blurted. And while that was blunt it wasn't the whole truth, but telling the man who had made it clear he did not and never would love her that he owned her heart was not on.

He smiled at her, the expression unguarded for just a moment so she saw the difference between his normal smiles and this one. "I *really* like your honesty, *kiska*."

Everything inside her seized with the need to claim this man. "I'll marry you."

His smile fell away, but he didn't look unhappy, just really serious.

Silently, he stood up from his seat, and then he moved around the table to take one of her hands to pull her to feet, as well. "Will you marry me, Lady Nataliya?"

She stared at him in confusion. She'd just said she would. Then she realized what he was doing. Giving her the proposal.

And something else clicked. He'd *always* planned to propose tonight. That little trinket box had been a hint, but he had *not* intended for it to be the question.

She liked knowing that. A lot. She'd told him she wanted a proposal and because it was something he could give her, he had done. "Yes, Your Highness, I would be honored to be your Princess."

Then he kissed her, despite there being bodyguards all around. It wasn't a chaste kiss either.

His mouth claimed hers, his tongue sliding between her parted lips to tangle with hers. It was like the other night, but not.

She felt absolutely connected to this man and his arms around her in this very public place proclaimed she was his, as he was hers.

The kiss went on for long moments until flashes behind her eyelids made her open her eyes and she realized they'd drawn the attention of some enterprising paparazzi as well as park visitors using their camera phones.

"We're going to be viral by tomorrow," she husked.

"You were agreeing to be my wife—I do not mind the entire world knowing that."

"Me either." She sighed. "But I think we've given them enough fodder for gossip."

"Do you think so?" He lowered his head and kissed her once more.

Because he wanted to show he wasn't ashamed of claiming her? Because he was too arrogant to let her call things to a halt? Just because he wanted to?

She didn't know and didn't care as she responded with a passion-filled joy she'd never thought to experience.

CHAPTER SEVEN

WHEN NATALIYA RETURNED to her hotel later that night, she called Mama to warn her about the formal announcement going out the next day.

Nikolai had never doubted Nataliya's answer even if he had been willing to ask the question.

"Are you sure this is what you want?" Mama asked, sounding worried.

"Why are you asking me that now? You didn't ask me ten years ago when I signed that contract if I was doing what *I* wanted." Nataliya didn't know where the words came from.

She sounded bitter, but she wasn't bitter. Was she? She'd never thought she was.

Her mother had done the best she could, but she hadn't been raised to stand up to family pressure, or even to stand against an abusive bully that called himself a husband.

Only it did feel like it was ten years too late to be asking Nataliya if she wanted to be a princess.

"Ten years ago, I was still desperate to go home, desperate to return to life as I knew it." Went unsaid was the truth that Solomia had been prepared to allow her daughter to pay the price to make that happen.

"And I was the conduit for that happening," Nataliya spelled out.

"You were born into a royal family—your life was never going to be entirely your own. No more than mine has been."

So, why ask if marriage to Nikolai was what Nataliya wanted now? "Did you ever want something different for me?"

"Why, when I believed that was the way life should be?" Her mother's sigh was clear across the phone. "I'm not the same woman I was ten years ago."

"So you don't still believe that?"

"If I could go back ten years, I would insist you *not* sign that contract," her mother said fiercely.

"Why?"

"Because at the time I didn't realize it could mean you would end up married to the King." And her mom's tone made that sound like the worst imaginable fate.

Nataliya didn't understand why. "Not because you didn't think an arranged marriage was a bad thing."

"No, actually. I didn't want you to love your husband like I loved your father. It made our relationship too inequal."

"You believe I love Nikolai like that," she said with dawning understanding.

Her mother was worried about Nataliya being hurt the way she had been.

"Don't you?"

"Nikolai is not anything like my father," she said instead of answering. Nataliya had never lied to Mother and she wasn't going to start now.

"You look at him with such fascination," her mother said, like that was a tragedy. "You always have done. Even before that contract. When the idea of you marrying Konstantin came along I thought I saw a way of protecting you from the pain of living with a one-sided love."

"Because you didn't think Nikolai could ever love me."

Her mother's scoffing sound was answer enough. And surprisingly hurtful. "He was infatuated with Tiana from the time he first laid eyes on her. They were of an age. She sexually enthralled him. I knew because I recognized the signs. I was enthralled with your father and I ended up badly hurt because of it."

"So you didn't want me to love my husband?" Nataliya asked with disbelief. "I think that's a little extreme."

"Not in the world I have always lived in. How many of our family's marriages are based on love, or even include romantic love, do you think?"

"Maks and Demyan both love their wives deeply."

"Your cousins have been very lucky and so have the women they married because incredibly, they share an abiding, reciprocal love."

"But you don't think any man would love me that way?" Nataliya asked painfully.

"My dear daughter, you are more comfortable with computers than people. You are no femme fatale, or even sexually aware socialite like Queen Tiana was. I love you with my whole heart—"

"But you don't think Nikolai ever will," Nataliya interrupted. "Well, that's fine. He wants me." She did not doubt that at all now. "And I want him. I don't need him to fall in love with me."

The secret hopes in the deepest recesses of her heart said otherwise, but no one else ever had to know about those.

"I sincerely hope for your sake, that is true. Just promise me..." She paused as if searching for words.

"Promise you what?"

"If he ever hurts you, with his fists or his infidelity, you will leave. The first time. Not the fiftieth."

As much as her mother's earlier words had hurt her, these showed just how deeply the Countess loved her daughter. Mama dove into the wedding preparations after that, insisting on flying to Mirrus and liaising with the official wedding planner in situ and Solomia planned to still be there when Nataliya arrived for her visit.

Home in Seattle, Nataliya was happy to discover that Nikolai continued to text and call as often as his schedule allowed.

He also continued to send what he now called betrothal gifts for her online auction. And that touched her in ways she wouldn't have admitted to anyone else. Even Jenna.

They made plans for Nataliya to travel to Mirrus so that she could spend time with him and his family before the wedding.

"You are aware that I have known your family for a

long time now," she said one evening on the phone as they discussed her upcoming trip.

"But not as my future bride. Both my father and brother need to come to terms with treating you like *The* Princess of Mirrus."

Nataliya wasn't surprised that neither the former King nor his second-eldest son, Prince Konstantin, were keen on her in the role. She'd offended them both and didn't regret that. So how could she regret that they *had to come to terms* with her as the future Princess of Mirrus?

"I notice you don't mention your younger brother," she teased, knowing full well that Dima liked her just fine.

"He thinks you're a goddess since you convinced me to allow him a gap year between the university and graduate school."

She laughed. "Does he know how easy that was?"

"And let him believe I'm *easy*? No chance."

"You'd prefer he think I have undue influence."

"Influence yes. Excessive amounts?" he asked with dismissive candor, no teasing in *his* voice. "Not likely."

He said stuff like that sometimes that made her think she needed to ask about his first marriage, but Nikolai clammed up whenever Tiana was mentioned in passing, much less asked about directly.

"Don't worry. I'm not in this for my influence over the King."

"Why are you in this?" he asked. Then sighed. "Forget I asked that. I know why you said yes to my proposal."

"You think so?"

"You would not go back on your word."

"So you think I said yes because I signed that contract?" she asked, wondering how he could be so blind to her feelings.

Of course she'd never voiced them, but he'd noticed her teenage crush when she'd thought she'd done a much better job hiding it than the love that she could no longer deny she felt for him.

"Why else?" he asked, as if there really couldn't be another reason.

And she had to smile, though he could not see it. "Because I want to be *your* wife."

"You are good for my ego." His voice was rich with satisfaction, but more than that, Nikolai really sounded pleased.

And she thought that was definitely worth admitting that much of the truth. "I don't think your ego needs inflating," she teased.

"You might be surprised."

"Nikolai?"

"Yes?"

"Were you happy with Tiana?"

Silence pulsed across the phones for long moments. Then he sighed. "At first, I was deliriously happy. Later, I regretted ever meeting Tiana much less marrying her."

Nataliya had to stifle a gasp of shock. "Your marriage looked so perfect from the outside. You grieved her death. I know you did."

"I did, but relief was mixed with the grief. And I lamented the loss of my unborn child as much, or more than, my wife."

"I'm sorry."

"I was too, but that time in my life is over. You and I will start a new chapter."

"We already have." It was no less than the truth. For both of them.

Despite the shortness of their engagement, Nikolai found himself unexpectedly impatient for the event in the weeks leading up to his wedding.

Far from assuaging his desire for his intended bride, the knowledge that she *would* be his soon only made him want her more.

He'd been surprised by how much he craved sex with Nataliya. Though lovely, she had none of the overt sensuality of Tiana, and the women shared almost nothing in common physically. Tiana had been a petite, curvy, blonde socialite. He'd *thought* she was his idea of sexual perfection.

Then he'd started looking at Nataliya as a potential bride and discovered that statuesque five-foot-nine innocence really did it for him. He could not wait to touch and taste her modest curves, to see how sensitive the nipples tipping her small breasts were. He wanted to touch the silky mass of her dark hair, to feel her body pressed all along his length.

She was going to fit him perfectly.

He had a purely atavistic anticipation of becoming Nataliya's first lover and spent more time fantasizing about their wedding night than he wanted to admit. He would certainly never allow Nataliya to know how much he wanted her.

He'd learned his lesson.

But that didn't mean he didn't crave her. He did.

Nikolai had never had a virgin in his bed. Though he'd believed his first wife to be untouched until their wedding night.

She'd laughed at his surprise, telling him not to be such a throwback.

And he had taken her criticism to heart, realizing that it would be wrong to expect something from her he had not himself practiced.

Because although he had never found uncommitted sex the tension relief that Konstantin did, Nikolai *had* had a few partners when he was at the university.

In fact, he'd thought he was sexually sophisticated until he had married.

Tiana had been an expert at using her sensuality to tie him into knots. Nikolai had made several decisions under the influence of his desire for her brand of sexuality.

He would never be so weak again.

His virgin fiancée was not going to play those kinds of games, he thought with a great deal of satisfaction. Even if Nataliya had enough sexual experience to know *how* to play the *tease and withhold* game, she would not do it.

It was not only in physical appearance that his future wife differed so strongly from the woman he had once made his Queen.

Nataliya had all the honor that Tiana had lacked.

Nataliya would *never* take bribes in exchange for influencing her husband's political or business decisions. She had even made it clear that their marriage would harbinger a shift in her loyalties from the Volyarussian royal family to *his* family and people.

Knowing how willing she had always been to sacrifice for the good of the Volyarussian monarchy, he found a great comfort in that truth.

Yes, Nikolai had made a very good decision when he determined to make Nataliya his Princess.

CHAPTER EIGHT

NIKOLAI SENT HIS personal jet to fly Nataliya to Mirrus for her visit.

That didn't surprise her. The social secretary and public relations consultant waiting on board for her did. Jenna had agreed to travel with her as her stylist.

The magazine was happy because Jenna was also doing a new series of articles on the personal fashions for *The* Princess of Mirrus, including an exclusive on her wedding dress and those of her attendants.

"We've both been hired on a trial basis, Lady Nataliya," the social secretary explained. "His Highness wants you to have final decision about the people who make up your team."

"Of course he does," Jenna said. She thought Nikolai pretty much walked on water.

Nataliya rolled her eyes at her friend. "Do you think I would tolerate anything else?"

"Well, you are fulfilling a draconian contract that most modern women would reject outright. Even if it is to marry King Yummy." Jenna waggled her eyebrows.

The PR consultant looked pained. "If we could refrain from mentioning the contract." She gave Jenna a stern look. "And from using terms such as *King Yummy*."

Unperturbed, Jenna just grinned. "Things like that contract don't stay secrets."

"The contract has never been a secret," Nataliya said with some exasperation. "And this modern woman is not naive enough to believe that everyone gets married for nothing but *true love*."

"That is true, but we would prefer the international media pick up on the romantic element to your relationship with His Highness," the public relations consultant said repressively.

"What romantic element?" she asked.

It was Jenna's turn to look pained. "Please, Nataliya. Even I can see the sparks that arc between you two when you are in the same room."

"That's chemistry, not romance," Nataliya maintained. She might love her fiancé, but she was under no illusion the feeling was mutual.

The PR consultant looked like maybe she was regretting taking this job. Even temporarily. "His Highness has engaged in a very romantic courtship, my lady."

"Nataliya, please."

The consultant gave Nataliya a slightly superior look. "It might be a good idea to get used to being addressed by your title, before you become The Princess of Mirrus."

Nataliya's mouth twisted with distaste, but she nodded. The other woman was right, but that didn't mean Nataliya had to like it.

However, she did have experience with formal protocol as part of the royal family of Volyarus. And she was not unfamiliar with being addressed as *lady*, simply not enamored of it. But she'd have to get over that and she knew it.

By the time they reached Mirrus, Nataliya's new social secretary had briefed her on how her visit to the small Russian country would go. As the future Princess of their King, she would be greeted on landing with a formal procession and would be attending not one, but three royal receptions in the five days of her visit.

Nikolai had been right. It would be very different from the times she had spent in Mirrus before.

If Nataliya had been hoping for more time getting to know the man she planned to marry, she realized that wasn't going to happen.

He was there, with the officials, when her plane landed however.

Her social secretary sighed, the sound someone makes after watching a really sweet movie. "His Highness is smiling."

Her gaze locked on Nikolai's handsome countenance, Nataliya could do nothing but nod. He *was* smiling.

Which she realized wasn't something he used to do. Like at all.

But during their courtship, he'd graced her with that slashing brilliance often. And she'd basked in the warmth of it. Even as she was not consciously aware of how uncommon it was.

"Oh, that will make good copy," the PR consultant said.

And Nataliya's answering smile slid from her face.

Nikolai's brows drew together, and he took what looked like an involuntary step forward.

"Good grief. Lay off with the PR perspective, would you?" Jenna demanded of the PR consultant as she shouldered past the other woman to stand right behind Nataliya. "He wasn't smiling at you for public relations. He's happy you're here, friend."

"This is not proper protocol," the PR consultant reminded them. "Your stylist should not be in position to have photos with you."

Nataliya turned her head to look at the PR consultant. "Jenna is my friend before anything else and as such she is always welcome in the frame with me."

The other woman shook her head, actually taking hold of Jenna's arm to pull her back. "She can be your *friend* but not in optics. She's not from Mirrus. She's not from the nobility. Miss Beals isn't the right sort of person for you to favor in the PR angle."

"Please, take your hand off of Jenna." Nataliya waited until the other woman complied. "We can discuss this later. I'm not sure your views and mine are on the same wavelength."

The look the other woman gave her said she agreed, but it wasn't the PR consultant who had it wrong. That was going to be a problem, but right now Nataliya needed to greet Nikolai.

She smiled and went down the stairs to the tarmac.

The King stepped away from the rest of the dignitaries and reached for her hand. "Welcome to Mirrus, Nataliya."

He didn't use her title and Nataliya's smile returned. "I'm very glad to be here. Nikolai."

Then he did something entirely unexpected. Nikolai leaned down and it seemed like he was about to kiss her.

Mesmerized by his nearness, she did not move. And then he *was* kissing her. In front of the dignitaries, the press and the special guests given permission to greet her plane.

All of those people faded from her consciousness as his lips played over hers. She leaned toward him and he let her, making no move to keep protocol-worthy distance between them.

Nikolai lifted his head, an expression of satisfaction stamped clearly on his features, but she did not understand its source.

"I think I'm going to have to let the PR lady go," she blurted. "We don't see the world through the same lens at all."

He nodded. "Okay."

"You don't mind?"

"Both she and the social secretary, Frosana Iksa, know they were hired on a provisional basis."

"The provision being that I approved them?"

"Exactly."

"I like Frosana. I think she'll make a good social secretary, but the public relations consultant called Jenna out for standing next to me."

"Jenna is your friend. Where else would she stand?" he asked, showing that he understood life was about more than strict protocol.

"Exactly."

And maybe the PR consultant could change her perspective to more reflect Nataliya's, but somehow she doubted it.

That was the last moment they had for anything resembling private conversation as she was introduced to cabinet ministers and the C-level management from Mirrus Global.

She noticed that neither Prince Evengi nor Prince Konstantin were present.

But Nataliya did not allow that to bother her. If they were making a statement, that was not her problem. If they were too busy, again, not her problem.

She wasn't marrying either of them and if they had anything to say about her becoming The Princess of Mirrus, that was between them and Nikolai.

Since he'd made it clear he wanted her to marry him, she trusted the savvy, modern King to know his own mind. And how to handle opposition from within his own family when it came.

There were even dignitaries in the car with them on the way back to the palace, but Nataliya was pleased to see that Nikolai had arranged for Jenna to ride with them as well, cementing in the minds of those present her friend's role and the respect the royal family expected to be accorded to the best friend of the future Princess.

Nataliya's mother was with Prince Evengi at the palace when they arrived, the pair looking thick as thieves as they went over wedding preparations in the drawing room.

Mama gave Nataliya a warm hug and kisses on both cheeks before doing the same for Jenna. "I'm so pleased you could be here to support Nataliya, Jenna. You're a good friend to my daughter."

Jenna hugged the Countess back. "Are you kidding? I'm living the fairy tale without any of the angst."

Mama laughed, but Prince Evengi looked inquiringly at Jenna. "You believe Lady Nataliya is living a fairy tale?"

"Well she is marrying a handsome king," Jenna said drolly, showing no discomfort at being addressed by a king, but dropping into a curtsy as Nataliya had taught her to do even as she answered so frankly. Then she tacked on, "Your Highness."

"Ah, the Countess has coached you in protocol. That will help both your and Nataliya's acceptance now and in the future."

"Actually, it was Nataliya. She's perfect princess material. But you knew that, or you never would have signed that contract ten years ago."

Nataliya had to hold back her laughter at the look of consternation on the King's face.

"So I have reminded my father more than once in the last weeks."

Nataliya was a lot more shocked by Nikolai's willingness to air discordance with his father in front of others than by his championship of her. He was too strong willed to ever tolerate even the former King's second-guessing his choice of wife.

"I believe you were the author of the articles on Lady Nataliya's foray into dating," Prince Evengi observed to Jenna.

"I was. It turned out to be a nifty bit of PR for your son's courtship of my friend."

"It did at that." He frowned. "But that was not the intention of that article, was it?"

"No. The intention of the article was to highlight first-date styles for each season."

"And here I thought it was to embarrass my younger

son into withdrawing from the contract," Prince Evengi said wryly.

"But how could that be when his older brother was not in the least embarrassed by the fact the woman he chose to court was attractive to other men?" Jenna asked innocently.

"You are quick on your feet," Prince Evengi said without a shade of irritation. "That will do you well if you choose to attend the receptions introducing Lady Nataliya."

"I'm invited?" Jenna asked, for once not sardonic, but surprised.

"Of course you are, dear," Mama inserted. "You are my daughter's best friend."

"I'm her stylist."

"Because she trusts you more than anyone else, or we would have a different stylist here for the week, but you still would have been invited to join her."

This was news to Nataliya, but she didn't doubt her mother's words. Mama was no longer the eager-to-please woman she had been when Nataliya was a child.

Prince Evengi took the news that Nataliya wasn't convinced the PR consultant would be a good fit with her with a frown, but one look from Nikolai and even the arrogant former monarch did not voice his evident displeasure.

"She came with the best of recommendations and had a great deal of experience working with royalty," Mama said musingly.

"I do not want a consultant who thinks every aspect of my life is a PR opportunity." Nataliya understood that her life had changed irrevocably when she agreed to marry Nikolai, but she was still a person in her own right with a life she intended to live happily.

"You have agreed to marry a king. Your life is no longer your own," Prince Evengi said but without reproach.

So, Nataliya did not take offence. Particularly since he only voiced her own thoughts. "No. It now belongs in a very real way to the people of Mirrus, but it will never belong to a PR consultant," Nataliya answered with spirit.

"And here I thought at least part of it belonged to me," Nikolai teased.

The varying looks of shock at his facetious comment made Nataliya smile. "Yes, just as yours belongs to me."

"But neither of us is willing to be bossed around by petty dictators masquerading as our personal staff." This time Nikolai's tone was nothing but serious and the look he gave his father and then the various staff members standing around left no one doubting he meant exactly what he said.

"Perhaps Gillian has someone she might recommend," Mama suggested. "I think you and she have similar viewpoints on the matter of public relations balanced with family and life."

Nataliya nodded to her mother's comment, her gaze caught by the look in Nikolai's gray eyes.

And for just a second, it was like they were alone in the room. Then Prince Evengi said something. Nikolai's expression veiled and a discussion of the finer details of the wedding ensued.

* * *

Nataliya and Nikolai did not have a private moment until after the formal dinner and reception that evening.

Nataliya had been introduced to a good portion of the Mirrus nobility, Prince Evengi doing the honors and exhibiting none of his reticence about her becoming the next Princess of Mirrus. Nataliya had met some of these people before when attending Nikolai's coronation and later Tiana's funeral, but of course they responded entirely differently to her in her new role.

There was a great deal of curiosity in the looks directed at her, though no one was gauche enough to give it voice.

But she *had* been intended for the second son and now she was marrying the King.

Despite the curiosity and the fact that formal functions had never been Nataliya's favorite thing, she managed to enjoy her evening. Mostly because while his father had taken on the role introducing her, Nikolai still contrived to be by her side for almost the entire evening, making it clear the wedding was not something he was being pressed into.

Nataliya and Nikolai were now walking in the private courtyard gardens. Nataliya found herself enchanted by them, lit beautifully to highlight the evening-blooming flowers and fountains.

"It's gorgeous out here." She had not seen this garden on her previous visits.

"My mother loved exotic flowers, not just orchids. She designed this garden as a private retreat for our family." Nikolai looked around as if remembering happy times. "There are both day- and night-blooming flowers."

"Don't they die in winter?" Nataliya asked while wondering what the gardens looked like during the day.

They were so magical now, she was almost afraid to see them and be disappointed.

"There is a retractable glass ceiling that is closed when temperatures drop."

"Amazing."

"And decadent, yes, but it made my mother happy and I find having a place in the palace that is reserved for family and only the closest of friends beneficial, as well."

"So, no using it to impress VIPs?" she asked, only half joking.

"No. Though my father argued doing just that many times with my mother, but she stood firm." Nikolai's smile was reminiscent.

"And he loved her enough not to gainsay her?" Nataliya asked, finding it difficult to imagine the arrogant former ruler in the role of adoring spouse.

"He respected her. I do not know if he loved her. That element of their relationship was not my business."

"He must have respected her a great deal not to start using it the way he wanted to once she was gone."

"Yes." Nikolai gave Nataliya a knowing look. "My mother was also formidable of nature. Much like someone else I know, she refused to be budged on matters that were important to her. I would not have put it past her to demand a deathbed promise from my father not to *desecrate* her garden."

Nataliya wished she'd had the chance to get to know his royal mother. She sounded like an amazing and strong woman. "Are you calling me stubborn?"

"Are you trying to imply you aren't?" he countered.

She shrugged. "You don't get far giving in." She'd learned that early.

"No, you do not."

"You're pretty stubborn yourself."

"And arrogant, or so you've said."

She couldn't deny it. "Was it all for PR?" Nataliya found herself asking, when in fact she'd had no intention of doing so.

Her mind had actually been on the promise she needed him to make her.

Nikolai led her to an upholstered bench with a back, its design in keeping with the Ancient Roman theme throughout the garden. He pulled her to sit beside him, the large central fountain in front of them, giving a sense of privacy that was probably false. But still, it was nice.

"Was what all for PR?" he asked her, genuine confusion lacing his voice. "I thought we'd just established this garden is not for public consumption, relations or otherwise."

Oops. "The PR lady said your courtship was a perfect romantic public relations coup."

"You are asking if my attempts at showing you how well suited we are were in some way motivated by a desire to look good for the public?" he asked, still sounding more confused than offended.

"Konstantin breaking the contract wasn't going to look good in the media." Nataliya sighed. "If I'd broken it, it wouldn't have looked any better. The press would have gone looking for the why and they might have found the same thing I did."

Nikolai looked surprisingly unworried by that prospect. "He might have been labeled the Playboy Prince, but I'm not as concerned about things like that as my father."

"You aren't?"

"No. I would be furious with either of my brothers if they married and then continued to play the field, but prior to marriage? I expect them only to behave with honor. And in answer to your question, no, my courtship of you was not a PR stunt."

"Courtship is a very old-fashioned word."

Nikolai's powerful shoulders moved in an elegant shrug. "In some ways, I'm a very old-world man."

She thought about his subtle change to her wording and smiled. "Yes, I think you are."

"In your own way, you are also very old-world."

She could not deny it. Perhaps it had been spending her formative years living with the volatile and pain-filled marriage of her parents, or simply being raised to respect duty and responsibility as paramount in her life, but Nataliya approached the world very differently than the friends she'd made in the States.

Even though she'd lived there more years than she had in Volyarus.

Nataliya's mouth twisted wryly. "Jenna calls the contract draconian."

"Haven't you thought the same thing?" he asked.

"Yes."

"But still, you honored it."

"My agreement to marry you had more to do with you than the contract," she told him with more honesty than might have been wise.

Nataliya had no intention of admitting her love for a man who didn't want it, but she wasn't going to have him believe she was more motivated by duty than she was.

Looking back, she wondered if she would have still backed out of the contract even if Konstantin hadn't proven himself to be a man she would never trust.

She could not imagine a wedding night with any other man than Nikolai.

"You do me a great honor saying so." The words were formal, but the look he gave her was heated.

Her body responded to that look in an instant, her nipples going hard and sensitive as they pressed against the silk of her bra. Nataliya pressed her legs together, the feelings in her core ones she'd only ever experienced with him.

The air around them was suddenly sultry.

"You have offered me the same assurance." Her voice came out husky and quiet, revealing the effect his intense regard was having on her. And there was nothing she could do about that.

They weren't kissing. Or talking about intimacy, but sexual desire was roaring through her body like a flash flood, drowning every other thought and emotion in its wake.

"You want me." His tone was filled with satisfaction laced by something like wonder.

Which made no sense. Considering what he knew of their history, he could not be surprised she wanted him.

Although the level of passion he drew out of her shocked even Nataliya.

She literally shook with the need to touch and to be touched by this man.

Nataliya leaned forward and tipped her head up so their lips were only a breath apart. "Of course I want you." And his unhidden desire for her only fed that craving until she had no choice but to act.

Pressing her hands flat against his chest, inside his suit jacket, so she could feel the heat of his body through the fine fabric of his shirt, she let her lips touch his.

He growled deep in his chest but made no move to take over the kiss.

Nataliya's fingers curled into the fabric of his shirt while she moved her lips against his, teasing the seam of his mouth with her tongue as he had done to her.

His lips parted and his tongue came out to slide along hers, but it was not enough. She needed more.

More touch.

More of his mouth against hers.

More of his body and her body together.

More.

More.

More.

She climbed onto his lap, her legs straddling his hard thighs, the soft silky fabric of her cocktail dress cascading around them in a rustle of silk.

She pressed down against the hard ridge in his trousers, the layers of cloth between her most sensitive flesh and his no barrier to sensation. Without conscious thought, she rocked against him, increasing that sensation, driving her own pleasure higher.

He groaned, hard hands clamping on her hips.

For one terrible moment, she thought he was going

to stop her, but he pulled her even closer, guiding her to a more frenzied rocking and suddenly she wasn't in control of the kiss anymore.

And she didn't care.

He knew exactly what she needed.

More of him.

And he gave it to her until the spiraling tension inside her made it almost impossible to breathe.

She broke her mouth from his. "Please, oh, please, Nik."

"Please what, *kiska*? Please this?" And one of his hands slid up her torso to her nape and then the hidden hooks holding the halter of her bodice together were undone and silk was sliding down bare and heated flesh.

Nipples already aching with arousal went so hard she hissed in borderline pain.

But he knew and he touched and squeezed and rolled and played before dipping his head to take one turgid nub into his mouth.

Nataliya cried out as ecstasy exploded in sparks through her.

Nikolai's mouth demanded nothing less than everything she had to give. And she gloried in the giving.

They rocked together, one of his hands on her hip and the other playing with her breasts. She kneaded his chest like the kitten he called her and gloried in the rising sensations.

Suddenly his hand on her hip moved to press against her bottom, increasing the pressure between their cloth-covered intimate flesh. His body went rigid and he groaned into their kiss like he was dying.

But he wasn't. He was experiencing the ultimate pleasure with her.

And knowing that was all her body needed to explode in the kind of ecstasy she hadn't known she could feel. Even after what she had already experienced with him.

These intense sensations were in a class all their own.

Her womb clenched and she knew that if he'd been inside her when this had happened, she would have gotten pregnant. It was too powerful not to have borne fruit.

She bit her lip and met his molten gaze. "And I can't wait for our wedding night. I used to think sex wasn't all that."

"You've never had it—how would you know?" he asked with an intimate smile.

"I never cared that I didn't have it," she told him. "And just because I never had sex with another person doesn't mean I didn't learn my own body's reactions."

"Hmm, I'd like to learn some more of your body's reactions." He frowned. "But not tonight." He looked around the garden. "I cannot believe we did that here."

"Do you regret it?" she asked.

"No." He helped her straighten her clothes. "But we are lucky we were not discovered. Although only family is allowed in these gardens, any one of them could have walked up on us."

"That would have been terribly embarrassing," she acknowledged, but she was still glad she had the effect on him that she did. "Sometimes I get the feeling you don't *want* to want me."

"Of course I do. Believe it, or not, but if I had not found you attractive, I would have found an honorable way around that contract."

"I believe it." But that didn't answer the truth that sometimes he said or did things that implied he refused to allow himself to desire her *too* much.

And maybe that was the key. The too much. Because Nataliya remembered how he used to look at Tiana. And there had been no tempering in the desire Nikolai had felt for his first wife.

Whatever had happened between the two, it had taught this proud King that sexual desire that went too deep was dangerous.

Putting those thoughts aside because she could not change his past, or her own for that matter, Nataliya focused on their future. "I need a promise from you before we marry."

"Yes?" Nikolai shifted Nataliya so she was sitting sideways on his lap, but still so close to him their body heat mingled.

"I need your word that you will be faithful." Nataliya loved both her mother and her Aunt Oxana, but she had no desire to live their lives.

"Haven't I already given it?" His patrician brows drew together. "I asked you to marry me. And a promise of fidelity will be included in our marriage vows."

"Yes, but I need you to promise me personally. To say the words and mean them."

"You know I keep my promises." There was no little satisfaction in his tone at that truth.

"I do."

"And you want this one?" Nikolai confirmed.

LUCY MONROE   143

"Among others."

"Very well," he said without asking what the other promises were. "I promise never to have sex with another woman while I am married to you."

"I promise never to have sex with another man," Nataliya offered, feeling something profound and right settle inside her.

His gray gaze flared with emotion and she knew she'd done the right thing.

Swallowing, Nataliya forced herself to continue. "I need you to promise that you would never physically hurt me, or the children we will have together."

She waited for Nikolai to get angry, but he didn't. He simply nodded.

"I promise to always use my strength to protect you and our children. I promise never to strike you. I promise you will always be safe with me." He was so serious and she could hear the sincerity lacing his deep, masculine voice.

"I promise you will always be safe with me, too." A person didn't have to be stronger, or bigger to hurt someone else. Only willing to do harm. And she wasn't.

CHAPTER NINE

THE REMAINDER OF Nataliya's visit to Mirrus went without incident, but there was also no repeat of the explosive passion in the garden.

She enjoyed meeting people at the receptions and was really happy with the plans in place for her wedding to the King. Her mom was over the moon about everything and that just added to Nataliya's sense of rightness about it all.

Yes, she had to live her life for herself, but knowing her choices were fulfilling some of her mother's dreams for her only child was nice.

Despite not being aware of Nikolai and Nataliya's time together in the garden, Prince Evengi and Mama contrived to make sure that Nikolai and Nataliya were not alone together for the remaining days of her trip.

Something Nataliya was seriously regretting as he escorted her to the airfield for her return to Seattle.

They were alone now; even Jenna was riding in another car, but the trip to the airport was not long enough.

"Are you sure you have to return to the States?" Nikolai asked.

His question startled Nataliya, because though he'd

made it clear he was looking forward to their marriage, he'd never intimated he wanted her to move to Mirrus any sooner than planned.

Nataliya frowned, her own disappointment in the answer she had to give riding her. "Yes. I've barely started packing up my things."

"We could hire movers."

She smiled, liking his enthusiasm, but shook her head. "No. I need to sort through stuff and decide what to do with my furniture." It would be silly to move all of her things only to discard half once they reached Mirrus.

"Donate it."

She laughed. "I think I'll post pics to social media first and make sure none of my friends want anything."

"Your friends would want secondhand furniture?" he asked, sounding just a little shocked.

And Nataliya had to laugh. "Yes, Nikolai. Plenty of people are happy not to have to buy a new kitchen table, or sofa."

"Surely it will not take three weeks to dispose of your furniture." His handsome features were cast in frustrated lines.

And she wanted to smile again, but she held back, thinking he might take her attitude the wrong way. But he was a king and this near petulance was charming. "It will take me two weeks to work out my notice and get together with my friends to say goodbye. I'm actually coming back the week before the wedding. I thought you knew that."

He made a dismissive gesture with his hand. "I am

glad of that, but I do not understand why you have to return to Seattle at all."

"I told you—"

"You have to work out your notice," he interrupted in a very unroyal-like way. "But Demyan will have to learn to do without you sooner, or later."

"In two weeks to be exact," she pointed out. "And there are still my friends."

"You're moving to Mirrus, not falling off the face of the earth. You do not have to say goodbye when surely it will be a see-you-again-sometime moment."

"For some, it may be. Like Jenna. But others I probably won't ever see again. Their lives and mine won't cross."

"Are you upset about that?" he asked.

"I'm a little sad naturally, but if I moved to another part of the country for my job the same thing would happen. Life is full of change."

"Your mother isn't happy we're getting married so quickly."

"But she is *thrilled* we are getting married. Mama will adjust to the timing of it."

Nikolai grimaced. "She pulled me aside and asked if I realized that our expedient marriage would give rise to gossip."

"She's probably right." They'd been over this, or had they? They'd talked about so much.

"You're not worried about it?"

"No. I'm not." Nataliya had learned long ago that she could either live in fear of the scandal mongers or ignore them. She chose to do the latter. "If we *had* anticipated our wedding vows and I had gotten pregnant, it would not have been a tragedy."

Nikolai looked startled at that. "Because people are already speculating?"

"That's one reason."

"And the other?"

"I would not be embarrassed to walk down the aisle pregnant with your child."

"You're something of a rebel in the royal family, aren't you?"

Nataliya shrugged. "Maybe? My experiences have taught me what is important."

"And gossip doesn't make it on the list."

"No."

"I will miss you, Nataliya." Nikolai gave her one of his genuine smiles, the ones that melted her. "I enjoy your company very much."

"I'll miss you too," she admitted.

He kissed her then, a soft, tender kiss that said goodbye and see you soon and I'll miss you.

She was still in a daze of emotional wonder when she boarded the plane and strapped into a seat beside Jenna.

"I think I'm going to have to break up with Brian," Jenna mused in a light tone at odds with her words.

Nataliya jerked her head around so she was facing her friend. "What? Why?"

"Because his kisses don't affect me like that."

"What kiss?"

"Please. Why else would His Highness have wanted you to himself if it wasn't to kiss you goodbye without an audience?"

"He did kiss me."

"I figured. You came on the plane in trance."

"I wasn't in a trance."

"Close enough." Jenna searched Nataliya's features. "I understand you agreeing to marry him better now though."

"Because I get a little spacey after he kisses me?"

"Because you love him."

Nataliya went still. "It's not a fairy tale, Jenna."

"No, but you love the King and he's pretty darn into you."

"He doesn't love me."

"Does that bother you?" Jenna asked, curiosity but not judgement on her face.

"It should, shouldn't it?"

"I don't know. If you were someone who wanted to marry for *true love*, maybe. But you're not. Even though they had an arranged marriage, your mom fell hard for your dad and he claimed to love her back, but that wasn't a recipe for happiness for any of you."

"No, it wasn't."

"Look, I get it. I'm not sure about the love thing, but I know I'd rather be in a relationship with a man who could kiss me stupid than a man who I don't miss when I'm away from him for almost a week."

"You really are going to break up with Brian."

"Yep."

"I *do* love Nikolai and I think he needs to be loved."

"Whereas you need to be respected and appreciated and I don't think anyone after these past few days is in any question how highly your future husband esteems you."

* * *

That esteem was put severely to the test a week later when Count Shevchenko gave a "tell all" interview that barely sideswiped the truth.

Yes, he was her biological father and yes she had signed a contract that included marriage between the two royal houses ten years ago.

But from that point it was pretty much fabrication and fantasy, and nasty fantasy at that.

Furious that he had not been invited to the wedding and even more angry that his daughter's elevation to Princess would not mean a lift of his own personal exile from Volyarus, the Count gave chapter and verse on the personal aspect to the contract signed ten years ago. He implied that Nataliya had not been content to marry a mere prince and had set her sights on the widowed King.

He painted his daughter as a scheming manipulator whose only interest was in her social position and wealth.

Nataliya was still reading the four-page spread in one of the most notorious gossip rags with international circulation when her phone's ringtone for Nikolai sounded.

Demyan, who had provided the paper and voiced support for her before she started reading, asked, "Is it King Nikolai?"

She nodded, having made no effort to pick up the phone.

"Are you going to answer it?"

Nataliya shook her head.

"Why?"

"I'm afraid."

"He's not going to call off the wedding because your father is a cretin."

"Won't he?"

Demyan grabbed Nataliya's phone and swiped. "No." Then thrust the phone at her.

She pressed it to her ear.

"Nataliya, *kiska*, are you there?" It was Nikolai's voice.

Of course it was Nikolai's voice. He didn't sound angry, but then he was a king. He didn't go around yelling when he got mad.

"Nataliya?" he prompted in an almost gentle tone. "I can hear you breathing. Say something, *kiska*."

"I..." She had to clear her throat. "I'm here."

"Are you all right?"

"Have you read it?" she asked in turn, without answering a question she actually wasn't sure she had an answer to. Was she all right?

Her father was doing his best to upend her life. Again. The last time he got her exiled from her country and her family. This time? Would he destroy her chance at marrying Nikolai?

A heavy sigh. "Yes, I have read it. I want you to come to Mirrus. I can protect you from the paparazzi here."

"You want me to come there?" she asked, trying to understand that request in light of how ugly the publicity was likely to get.

"You are not a little girl, Nataliya. He cannot destroy your life again. No one will ever take your home or family from you again. I will not allow it."

"I don't have a home." She wasn't even sure where

the words came from, except a tiny part of her heart that still held the wounds from her childhood.

Seattle had been her home for the last fifteen years, but her apartment was almost empty now, in preparation for her move to Mirrus. Only would Mirrus be her home now? After the article?

"He won't have only this up his sleeve," she warned Nikolai. "My father's probably planning to do a televised interview too."

"Your home is now the Palace in Mirrus and soon you will be my Princess. He can say what he likes, but nothing will change that."

"But he's always going to be a problem." She realized now how true that was.

Her father had no intention of staying quietly in the background. Apparently, he had no qualms about how he achieved the spotlight either.

"We will determine a plan of action for dealing with the Count, but I don't want *you* dealing with the intrusiveness of the media without my support."

Picturing just how intrusive things could get, Nataliya could feel the color draining from her face. Would the honorable thing to do be to withdraw entirely from her connection to Mirrus? And even her own royal family?

Her thoughts started spiraling and Nataliya felt dizzy with them.

"What's he saying?" Demyan demanded, putting his hand on her back and encouraging her to lean forward. "Breathe, Nataliya. Just concentrate on breathing."

"Hold on a second, please, Nikolai," she said into

the phone as she attempted to take a couple of deep, calming breaths.

He cursed. "You are not all right."

Nataliya just took another breath as the world came back into focus. She sat up, all the while aware that Nikolai was barking out orders to someone on his end of the phone.

"You can call back later, if this is a bad time," she offered.

"Nyet. No. Do not hang up on me, *kiska*."

"Okay." She looked at Demyan and wondered what he was making of all this.

Her cousin's expression was grim, but he reached out to squeeze her shoulder. "It is going to be okay, Nataliya."

She just shrugged, not at all sure he was right.

"Put me on speaker, please, *kiska*."

"Why?" One of the protocols all the royals learned early was never to use the speaker function on their phones. Too easy to be overheard.

"I can hear Prince Demyan," Nikolai said. "I'd like to speak to him too."

She still thought it was odd, but Nataliya did as requested.

"What is going on?" Demyan demanded toward the phone.

But Nataliya answered. "Nikolai wants me to go to Mirrus, to avoid the media."

Something like relief flitted over her cousin's hard features. "That's a good idea."

"I'm not running away." Her father wasn't going to make her abandon her job or her plans.

She wouldn't let him.

"Coming home is not running away," Nikolai opined.

"Be reasonable, Nataliya," Demyan added. "The vultures aren't going to let you go to the grocery store without incident, much less anywhere else."

"I have commitments throughout next week." She took another deep breath and let it out slowly, reminding herself that she was not a little girl to be pushed around by her father's whims. "I'll be fine. I'll stay at Mama's." She'd been planning to do that anyway, for her last couple of days in Seattle, as the shelter she was donating her bed to was scheduled to pick it up then.

"But your mother is not there. She is here. And her home is not secure."

"Her condominium is in a gated community. They even have security that do rounds."

"A rent-a-cop in his golf cart?" Demyan snorted derisively.

Nikolai was worryingly silent.

"Nikolai?" she prompted when he had not replied several seconds later.

"Yes, *kiska*?"

"I'm going to be fine but thank you for worrying about me." She had a lot of thinking to do and she knew she wouldn't make an unbiased choice if she went to Mirrus.

She couldn't simply consider what she wanted, but what was best for Nikolai and the people of Mirrus.

"You will be fine, yes. Demyan, please keep Nataliya inside the building until I arrive."

"Arrive? What do you mean arrive? You can't just drop everything and come here."

"Are you coming to Mirrus?" he asked.

"In a week." Maybe. "Nikolai, we need to think about how best to handle this and it might not be me coming to Mirrus in the near future." Or at all.

Demyan made a sound of disagreement.

Nikolai cursed again and then said, "I will see you in a few hours."

"But, Nikolai, there's no need." How was she supposed to make her mind up to break things off if he was there, tempting her?

"I know what you are thinking, Nataliya *moy*, and it is not going to happen. We are not breaking the contract. You are not backing out of this marriage." There was not a bit of give in Nikolai's aristocratic tones. "Prince Demyan?"

"I'll keep her inside, Your Highness."

Nataliya gave her cousin a look, but he just shrugged. "It makes sense, Nataliya, and you know it."

"Nikolai, you must realize that my uncle will want me to cancel the wedding to avoid further scandal," Nataliya said.

Demyan's grimace said he agreed.

"I repeat, we are *not* canceling our wedding," Nikolai said forcefully. "Any attempt to make you pay for your father's actions will be met with not only my disapproval, but retaliation."

Instead of looking annoyed by Nikolai's threat, Demyan grinned. "Good."

Nataliya was still trying to process that her fiancé was *not* looking for the easy way out of the scandal. Would not even hear of Nataliya backing away from their betrothal.

He'd been pretty adamant all along, but she found it incomprehensible Nikolai wasn't even considering it in the face of her father's behavior and the potential ugliness to come.

"I will see you in a few hours, Nataliya."

Nikolai and his larger-than-normal security team stepped off the elevator on the top floor of the Yurkovich-Tanner building in Seattle.

Prince Demyan was waiting, no doubt having been apprised of Nikolai's arrival. "She's in her office. Working."

The other man's tone let Nikolai know what he thought of that state of affairs and it wasn't approval.

"That sounds like Nataliya."

The Prince grimaced, but nodded. "My cousin has a full ration of our family's stubbornness."

"I have noticed."

"She'll pretend she's fine, but she's taking this hard," Prince Demyan warned as he turned to go down a soft carpeted hall. "Follow me."

Nikolai's security team took up different positions in the hall until only one remained at his side.

"That is to be expected," Nikolai said to Prince Demyan as they walked. "It is her father after all."

"Trying to ruin her life. The bastard."

"Indeed."

The Prince stopped outside a door and turned to face Nikolai. "You won't let her down, will you? She's going to try to sacrifice her own future for the greater good. I know her."

Prince Demyan's expression didn't bode well for

Nikolai if his answer was anything but no. It didn't worry Nikolai because he had no intention of letting the very special woman be hurt any more than she had already been by her father's reprehensible behavior.

And she was going to be his Princess.

"You mean like she did ten years ago when she signed that contract."

"Yes."

"She wants to marry me." Of that Nikolai was entirely convinced.

"I agree, but are you going to let her go?"

"Never," Nikolai assured the other man. "I will stand by her as her own family did not all those years ago."

Prince Demyan nodded, his expression grim, nothing to indicate he had taken offense at Nikolai's words. "Our King did not do well by her or the Countess."

"No, he did not."

The Prince's demeanor stiffened. "Fedir and Oxana have made decisions that were difficult for the good of our country." As their unofficially adopted son, Demyan had always had leave to use the familiar address for the King and Queen.

"Even so, it is not a decision you would have made." Prince Demyan could be entirely ruthless, hence his marriage to the one woman who could have destabilized the economy of Volyarus, but he was fiercely loyal.

And Nikolai had learned that the Prince had ensured his wife-to-be was more than adequately protected with their prenuptial agreement. He was not the type of man to allow someone else to suffer unfairly.

Prince Demyan inclined his head and offered more

truth than Nikolai was expecting. "Or that my adopted brother would make as sovereign."

"I believe that." Nikolai had done his homework on the entire family when he became King and his brother's betrothal became his responsibility and not that of their father.

"But that does not mean our King acted out of anything but duty and the belief that he was doing what was best for Volyarus."

"It would seem loyalty is a family trait."

"Nataliya is very loyal," Prince Demyan said, proving he knew exactly what Nikolai had meant.

Nikolai nodded. "It is one of the many things I admire about her."

"Good." The Prince opened the door and stood back to allow Nikolai entry.

Nataliya looked up from her computer, her face pale, her eyes haunted. "Nikolai! You're here."

"I told you I would be." He could only hope that his stubborn fiancée would cooperate with Nikolai's plan for dealing with the problem of her father.

"But you must have gotten on a jet almost immediately."

"I did." He instructed his remaining guard to wait outside the door and then closed it on him and her cousin.

Nataliya looked at the closed door with a worried expression. "I think Demyan wanted to talk strategy."

"You and I will do so. After."

"After?"

He crossed the room and pulled Nataliya from her chair and right into his body. "After we have greeted properly, and I have assured myself that you are all right."

"I'm fine."

He just shook his head and then kissed her.

She melted into him, no resistance whatsoever, kissing him back, her arms coming up and around his neck. Passion flared between them as it always did when they were this close, but he could sense a fragility in her that was not usually there.

And it was that fragility that allowed Nikolai to lift his head. "You are such a temptation, but I do not think you are fine at all."

"He said horrible things about me. I never did anything to him, but he never loved me." Nataliya snuggled into Nikolai, seeking comfort in a way that was both surprising and welcome. "I thought he couldn't hurt me anymore, but he can, and I don't like it. Mama will be so hurt. She's moved on with her life, but he's going to dredge everything up again. All the old pain while heaping on a new dose. It's just not fair."

"You have not spoken to her?" Nikolai knew the Countess had planned to call her daughter.

Nataliya shook her head. "I couldn't. She'll be devastated and it's all my fault."

"None of this is your fault," Nikolai argued, fury filling him that his sweet and loyal fiancée could take the blame for her reprobate of a father's actions. "All culpability lies one hundred percent with the Count."

Nataliya didn't answer, just leaned more securely into Nikolai, as if seeking strength. "I can't believe you came."

He was more than happy to share his with her, but

knew she had plenty of her own "I cannot believe you would think I would do anything else."

"But your schedule." Her head tucked perfectly under his chin, like she was made to fit against him like this.

"Can be adjusted," he reminded her. Nikolai rubbed her back, finding the action soothing and hoping she did too. "Just as yours must be."

Her head came up at that. "You're going to insist I return to Mirrus with you, aren't you?"

"I am hoping you have reconsidered that course of action on your own."

"And if I haven't?" she tested.

"I will leave it up to you to explain to my cabinet and my company why I am in Seattle when I am supposed to be in the palace for several important meetings prior to our wedding."

"You can't stay here!"

"I will not leave you alone to face the vultures of the press."

Nataliya sighed. "Demyan already told me that I didn't have a job to come to anymore."

"Did he?"

Her cousin went up a notch in Nikolai's estimation and he already respected the Prince.

"He said I was being recklessly stubborn."

"And what do you think?"

"I think you're both ignoring the most expedient course of action and I cannot figure out why. And in any case, I don't want to feel like a coward."

"There is nothing cowardly about coming home." He completely ignored her reference to expediency.

Their definition of that course of action wasn't going to match.

"And Mirrus is my home now?" she asked, her expression unreadable.

"You know it is."

She nodded and something in his chest loosened. "It is." She looked away from him. "I never thought I was weak, but I want to go back with you. I want to go through with the wedding."

Hearing the last loosened the remaining fear he had not wanted to acknowledge. She was not going to walk away from him. "No one could make the mistake of thinking you are weak," he promised her.

"You don't think so?" Nataliya was looking at him again, her lovely brown eyes shiny with emotion.

"No, but if they do, they are idiots."

"Why would a father be so cruel to his only child?" she asked, like she expected Nikolai to have the answer.

He didn't; he only had the truth he knew. "I am sorry, *kiska*, but your father is a cruel man all around. As to why the articles and why now, I do not think it is as simple as him wanting revenge for his continued exile."

That seemed to startle her. "What then?"

"Money."

"You think he hopes to extort money from us? But if that was the case, wouldn't he have threatened before going to the tabloids with his ugly allegations about my character?" Wasn't that how blackmail worked?

"He has done one interview in print, an interview that has forced everyone involved to sit up and take notice. As you said earlier, he could do much more, but right now he believes his bargaining position is strong."

"But blackmail? He couldn't think he'd get away with it. With King Fedir, that might even fly. After all, there's a reason my father has been able to draw his allowance from the family coffers annually, but with you? He must know you will never pay him a penny."

Nikolai liked very much that she knew him that well. "You do not think so?"

"No." She rolled her eyes. "He'd have better luck getting blackmail payments out of a nun who'd made a vow of poverty."

"Interesting analogy, but you are right." Nikolai had plans where her father was concerned and not one of them included paying a single penny to the grasping Count.

"You're talking like you know the Count wants money."

"I do know. He made the demand while I was en route."

Nataliya's natural lovely tone went paste white. "What does he want?"

"Right now? A single large payment followed by a yearly stipend to ensure his silence in the future. He's getting none of that," Nikolai assured her.

Before Nataliya could respond, a knock sounded at the door.

"Come," Nikolai commanded.

It opened to reveal the Prince. "Your guests are waiting in the lobby."

CHAPTER TEN

NATALIYA TRIED TO step back from Nikolai, but he wasn't having it. His arms remained firm around her as she tried to make sense of what her cousin had said.

"You never react like I expect you to," she told Nikolai.

Her proper King, who was known for his dignified demeanor, winked at her. "Just think, you will never grow bored with me."

There was an underlying seriousness to his teasing that Nataliya wished she understood better.

She patted his muscular chest, feeling daring with her cousin standing right there. "No chance of that happening."

"If we could suspend this somewhat nauseating chit-chat, everyone is waiting," Demyan said sardonically from his place in the doorway.

"Give us a minute," Nikolai instructed her cousin.

Demyan nodded and left.

"Are you ready?" Nikolai asked her.

"Ready for what exactly?"

"We're about to give a press conference."

"What? Why?"

"We're going to detooth the tiger."

"But my uncle." No way had King Fedir agreed to such a thing.

"Is not the sovereign in charge here."

But King Fedir could be impacted in a very detrimental way. There was a risk her uncle's own long-hidden scandal would come out if her father decided to exact revenge, though she wasn't sure Danilo would risk losing what income he still received from the Volyarussian royal coffers.

Either way, her former King's actions were no more her responsibility than her father's had been.

"What is that sound you made?" Nikolai asked her, as if they weren't in the middle of an intense discussion.

"Surprise," she answered, with no thought of hiding her thoughts from him. "I just thought of my uncle as my former King."

"I am your King now." Pure satisfaction laced Nikolai's tone.

She smiled, her heart beating fast for no reason. Or maybe for every reason. "Yes."

"It is my honor and my privilege to protect you and your mother as members of my family. And I will do a better job than your former King."

"Your arrogance is showing again."

"Perhaps. Will you do the press conference with me?"

"You're asking me?"

"I am."

"Yes, but I'm not sure what we are supposed to say?"

"In this one instance, I would consider it a personal favor if you would follow my lead."

"Okay."

"There's something else."

"What?"

"Beyond the press conference, we have two legal options open to us. We can file criminal charges against the Count for blackmail. Even if he has a good lawyer, he'll spend some time in prison. In addition, you can sue for libel and drag him through the courts for the foreseeable future. We don't have to win the case to bankrupt him with legal fees. He lives beyond his means as it is."

For the first time, Nataliya had hope her father would not prevail. Why hadn't she considered legal recourse?

Because to do so would cause scandal, and that was anathema to the Royal Family of Volyarus, but there was no way past scandal in this situation. Even paying the blackmail wouldn't guarantee her father's silence. He was vindictive and cruel and not always smart.

He could get angry and do something that would harm himself more than her or Mama in the end, but it would still harm them. Just as his actions had with their exile.

"He could go to prison?"

"All calls to the palace and to my personal cell phone are recorded."

Which meant that they had recorded evidence of the attempt to extort the King. "He should have gone to prison for what he did to my mom when they were married. He's broken the law again and I think he should pay the consequences of that, but I need to talk to my mother before I decide."

"I would expect no less from you. The charge doesn't become any less serious waiting a day or two to file."

Nikolai cupped Nataliya's cheek. "You understand that in trying to blackmail *me*, that even if we do not file a complaint here in the US, he is already guilty of treason against the Mirrusian Crown. If he ever attempts to enter our country, he will be detained, tried and most likely end up incarcerated."

Nikolai could have no idea how good that news sounded to Natalia.

Detooth the tiger indeed. "And the press conference?" she asked.

"We will set the story straight."

Jenna arrived then, for moral support, but also to help Nataliya get ready to face the press.

Again, Nikolai had thought of everything.

When they reached the lobby, both Nikolai's security and that for Yurkovich-Tanner were in position. There was a table covered with a cloth and bunting in the colors of the House of Merikov. The Mirrusian Royal Crest was displayed prominently on the front.

The cavernous lobby was packed. News crews from the major networks were there along with journalists for reputable entertainment shows, magazines and newspapers.

Demyan stood to one side, along with people Nataliya did not recognize.

One of those people stepped forward, introduced themself as the press liaison for King Nikolai of Mirrus, thanked everyone for coming, gave a few instructions for holding questions and the like and then introduced Nikolai and Nataliya.

"I want to thank you all for coming," Nikolai said

in confident tones. "Understandably my fiancée, Lady Nataliya of Volyarus, has been deeply saddened and upset by the spurious interview given by her father, the disgraced Count Shevchenko."

Nikolai smiled reassuringly down at Nataliya and whether it was for show or because he cared about her feelings in that moment, she felt better.

"The one thing the Count got right was that there was in fact a contract. Neither my people, nor King Fedir has ever tried to hide that fact."

Murmurs erupted in the room, but soon died down as it became obvious Nikolai would not continue until there was silence.

"That contract was not between Lady Nataliya and my brother."

"But she was expected to marry him?" a bold reporter called out.

He was shushed, but Nikolai answered. "That contract was signed ten years ago. If they intended to marry, I think it would have happened by now, don't you?"

Laughter erupted into the room.

Nikolai waited until it calmed down before going on. "The truth is that when I realized I'd mourned my deceased wife long enough, I looked around me and Lady Nataliya was the woman I saw."

Nataliya did her best to keep her smile and not show the shock she felt on her face. Did he mean that, or was it part of the damage control?

"My brother made his disinterest in fulfilling the contract official, leaving the way open for me to court the woman I wanted to stand beside me, but make no mistake, I had every intention of stealing Nataliya from my brother if he did not step aside."

Gasps sounded throughout the room, and the tap of furious typing on touch screens.

Even knowing how that all had come to pass, Nataliya almost believed Nikolai's version.

"So, the idea that Nataliya set her sights on me because I am a king when she was promised to my brother is a total fiction. The fact is, it was entirely the other way around. I set my sights on her and I courted her with every intention of success."

"How do you feel about that, Lady Nataliya?" a female reporter asked.

"Honored. And very pleased with the outcome. Anyone who thought Prince Konstantin and I would have a made a good couple doesn't know either of us very well."

"You don't like the Prince?" someone asked.

"I'll like him just fine as a brother-in-law," she promised.

Laughter erupted again.

The rest of the press conference was more of the same, and Nataliya's sense of unreality grew. How much of what Nikolai said was the truth and how much was *spin*? When the courtship had first started, it would not have mattered to her, but now?

Now that she realized she loved him, the answer to that question was of paramount importance.

More reporters and cameramen congregated on the walk outside the Yurkovich-Tanner building. These weren't the ones invited to the press conference. These were the ones who had read that sleazy interview with her father and wanted their pound of flesh.

Nataliya could see them from her seat beside Nikolai in the helicopter as it lifted off from the roof. They were traveling via helicopter rather than the jet he had arrived in because he had refused to allow her to be exposed to the clamoring press waiting like jackals.

She couldn't help feeling a certain satisfaction knowing the vultures had been deprived of their prey.

Not all journalists were bottom feeders. In fact, she was of the opinion *most* weren't. Her best friend being a prime example, and she'd been impressed by those who had shown up for the press conference.

But the ones hoping to get a word from, or a picture of, the scandal-tainted Lady Nataliya were the type who gave journos a bad name.

The rest of Nataliya's things were being packed up by movers and would be taken to Mirrus the following morning. Her social secretary, Frosana, was busy either canceling her final engagements with friends or rescheduling virtual get-togethers from the palace.

As they flew over the sea's choppy waters and Nikolai worked on his computer, dialing into meetings via a live feed from his laptop, Nataliya realized that her life had finally changed irrevocably.

The wedding was just a formality.

She no longer worked for Yurkovich-Tanner. Nataliya no longer lived in her own pretty condominium she had bought with her own money. She could no longer meet Jenna at their favorite coffee shop.

Nataliya would never again go shopping on her own, or go hiking by herself, or do anything alone again. Not really. Even when there was the illusion of privacy, it would only be that. An illusion.

From this point forward, she would always have a security detail. Though the wedding had not yet happened, she was already considered a part of the Royal House of Merikov.

Nataliya didn't have the title of princess yet, but this flight represented the end of her personal independence.

Maybe that was why she'd fought against going to Mirrus ahead of schedule.

Nataliya knew that this time, when she stepped foot on Mirrus soil, her entire life would change. Permanently.

Because of the man sitting beside her.

Her father had really picked the wrong victim when he'd tried to blackmail King Nikolai Merikov.

If there was a more stubborn person, as certain of his course, Nataliya had never met him.

Nikolai had decided that Nataliya would make a good wife and Princess to his people. And he had allowed no one to dissuade him, not his family, not his advisors, not even Nataliya herself.

Certainly, he wasn't going to allow a man like Count Danilo Shevchenko to undermine the King's plans.

Nataliya wasn't sure what Nikolai would make of her love for him, but she was sure it wasn't part of his plan.

Affection? Yes. She could see he wanted that, but a more consuming emotion? No.

Definitely not on his agenda to give or receive.

At first that had given Nataliya a sense of peace, but as her love grew she realized how difficult it would be to keep it to herself.

Especially when he acted like he had today, like her comfort and safety were *the* top priority. When he refused to give in to pressure and take the *easy* way to anything if it wasn't the *best* way.

He was such an honorable man.

Such a good man.

"What?" he mouthed to her.

"I'm fine," she assured him, knowing he would be able to read her lips, as well.

They weren't talking via the internal communication headsets because he was using his headset for the meeting he was dialed into via his laptop.

He clicked something and then his voice came through her headset. "You sighed."

"I did?" He noticed? While in a meeting?

"You did."

"Just realizing everything is different now."

"Everything became different the moment you agreed to marry me."

That was true. "But that difference wasn't real."

"And now it is?"

"Yes."

"Good."

She laughed. "No commiseration?"

"I am pleased you realize the weight of our choices. Your sense of honor and commitment are exemplary."

"You're such a sweet-talker," she said, tongue in cheek.

Unbelievably, color burnished his aristocratic cheeks. "I am not a romantic man." He said it like he was admitting a grave shortcoming.

Nataliya smiled, but shook her head. "I disagree.

You put on a very romantic courtship, but even if you hadn't? Believe me, I could not imagine a more romantic gesture than for you to clear your schedule and come to Seattle to bring me home."

The press conference had been pretty amazing too. He'd done something she knew her uncle wouldn't have.

"You didn't sound like you thought I was being romantic this morning."

"I was still fighting the final change to my life, I think," she admitted.

His brows drew together, like the idea of fighting one's duty was incomprehensible. "You knew it was coming."

"In two weeks."

"You're a little set in your ways, aren't you?" he asked like he was just now realizing that fact. "Not fond of change."

Her smile was self-deprecating. "Yes, I can be. Change is inevitable but not always my friend."

"This change will be good."

"If I didn't believe that, I wouldn't have agreed to marry you." She gave him a reassuring smile. "And please don't think I need romantic dinners in the park to be happy. The way you stood up for me today? The way you wouldn't let anyone make me a scapegoat for my father, even when I thought I needed to, that's the kind of romance that secures affection for a lifetime."

It wasn't the declaration of love her heart longed to make, but it was more than she thought she'd admit before the day's events.

"I can hope situations like that do not arrive often, but be certain I will always take your part."

"I believe you." And that? Was kind of amazing.

She trusted him in a way she trusted no one else. Not even her mother, whom Nataliya adored.

"I am glad."

Nataliya noticed one of the men at the conference table on the laptop's screen waving like he was trying to get Nikolai's attention.

"I think they need you." She indicated his computer. "I'm fine on my own."

He nodded and clicked back to his meeting without another word, trusting her at her word and Nataliya realized she really liked that too.

CHAPTER ELEVEN

THE DAYS LEADING up to her wedding were much busier than Nataliya had expected. Since she hadn't planned to be in Mirrus for several days, the fact she magically had a full schedule was another reality check.

Nataliya had always been aware that being a princess, especially The Princess of Mirrus, was a job. What she was coming to see was how much someone in her position had been needed.

The fact she was on call to Mirrus Global for her specialized computer skills took up some of her time, but so far she hadn't been pulled into anything really tricky or time-consuming.

She saw almost nothing of her fiancé during the day, their schedules both full without overlap. They dined together every evening, but even the dinners that were not State business offered no opportunity for her and Nikolai to talk privately.

He insisted on them spending an hour together each evening in the palace's private garden, but they never repeated the passionate kisses they had shared before she'd returned to Seattle.

She wasn't sure why.

It wasn't because he didn't want her. The sexual tension between them only got higher and higher as their wedding approached.

Nataliya didn't have enough experience with this sort of thing to know exactly what to do with that, but one thing she was not? Was a shrinking violet.

So, one evening a couple of days before the wedding, while they sat in the garden talking, like they had every evening for the past week, she reached over and laid her hand on his thigh.

Nikolai's reaction was electric. Her soon-to-be husband jumped up and moved several feet away before spinning around to face her. "What are you doing?"

Since she thought the answer to that question was more than obvious, Nataliya frowned and tried to make sense of his overblown response. "What's going on, Nikolai? I thought we agreed there was nothing wrong with sharing our passion?"

"We did." He looked like he was in physical pain.

She let her gaze slide over him and couldn't miss the erection pressing against his slacks. Did it hurt?

"Stop that!" he admonished.

"Stop what? Looking at you?" she asked with disbelief.

"Yes!"

This was just getting stranger and stranger. "Why?"

"I promised your mother," he gritted out.

"Promised Mama? That I wouldn't look at you?" That didn't make any sense.

"That I would not touch you again before our wedding night," he ground out.

Irritation filled Nataliya, both at her mother for asking for such a thing and at Nikolai for agreeing to it. "At all?" she clarified.

He shrugged.

"What does that mean?" She made no effort to hide the annoyance in her tone.

He winced. "It means that I'm on a hair trigger here. If I touch you or allow you to touch me, if I kiss you…" He visibly shuddered at the thought. "This thing between us is going to explode and I will break my promise."

"That you made to *my mother*?" Nataliya's voice held a wealth of censure. "*Why* did you make that promise?" He was too smart not to have known what a challenge it would be to keep.

For both of them.

"Because she asked me to."

"And that was enough?" Nataliya's voice rose on the last word.

The look he gave her from his steely gray eyes implied she should understand. "She's your mother."

"And *I'm* the one you are going to marry."

"Yes."

"So, why promise my mother something you had to know I would not like? Something that would be so difficult for us both?"

"At the time, I did not think you would be here on Mirrus until a couple of days before the wedding. It did not seem like a hardship."

"And now?"

He scowled, the look close to petulant.

"Not as easy as you thought, huh?"

"I would not make such a promise now."

"You thought, easy way to win some points with the future mother-in-law," she teased, her irritation evaporating, if not her sexual frustration.

"Something like that."

Even kings worried if their mothers-in-law approved. Who knew?

Even so. "You're usually better at foreseeing the potentially bad outcome. You didn't think, hey, this could backfire on me?"

"First, I do not think *hey* anything. Second, no, I did not foresee the potential for backfiring."

"You'd better have a pretty spectacular wedding night planned," she warned him.

His smile was devastating. "You are very demanding for a virgin."

"Maybe I wouldn't be so demanding if I had any choice about that status changing before our wedding," she grumbled.

"You could always seduce me," he offered.

She tilted her head to one side, studying him. "And that would not make you feel like you broke your promise?"

His expression said it all.

"That's what I thought." She nodded and then promised, "I will never knowingly undermine your integrity."

An arrested expression came over his aristocratic features. "That means a great deal to me."

"Why?" She shook her head. "I don't mean it shouldn't." She paused. "I think it just surprises me that you would not have taken it as given."

"There was a time when I did, but I learned I could not."

"With Queen Tiana?" Nataliya asked, bewildered by the possibility.

They had seemed so in love, but maybe she needed to rethink her belief on that.

"Da."

"You so rarely mention your first marriage." In the beginning, Nataliya had believed that was because he still grieved the loss of his wife.

Now, she wasn't so sure.

"Tiana was not above using her position as my wife and confidant for her own gains." Nikolai's voice was devoid of emotion.

But that confidence had to have cost him, in terms of pride, if nothing else. Nataliya could not wrap her head around his deceased wife using him, much less her position, in that way.

"That shocks you," he opined.

"Yes."

"Because you could not imagine doing such a thing."

"No." There was no point Nataliya trying to prevaricate. If it made her sound provincial rather than royal, that could not be helped.

"I believe you. And that makes me very happy." His tone wasn't lacking in inflection now. It positively rang with satisfaction.

Nataliya smiled, pleased that in this way at least he saw her as superior to the beauty he had married. "I'm glad."

"We are going to have a good marriage." He sounded very sure of that.

But that was nothing new. He'd been certain from the beginning. It was Nataliya who had taken some convincing.

"With a really special wedding night."

His sexy laughter followed her into her dreams that night and she woke with a sense of hope and happiness that only increased as Nikolai played out the humorous role of paying the bride ransom the day before their official ceremony. Because of the security necessary and the guests who would be attending their wedding, some traditions were more royal than orthodox.

Nataliya wore a vintage gown for the wedding. Despite its short lead-up time, the affair had dozens of the world's elites as guests.

The other couple of hundred guests were by no means to be dismissed. Nearly the entire nobilities of both Volyarus and Mirrus were in attendance, along with billionaire business associates.

Jenna was there, and although she would cover the wedding in an article she would write later, her only role at present was that of maid of honor or *witness* according to the traditions of the church.

Nikolai's *witness* would be his brother Konstantin, which had been suggested by the fixer to show the younger man's support of the proceedings despite being the one Nataliya had first been intended to marry according the contract. Nataliya didn't really care who stood up with Nikolai.

She was simply happy Jenna would be by *her* side at the wedding. Mama still insisted on calling it a *crowning* according to church tradition, because of the religious crowns placed on both her and Nikolai's heads during the ceremony. Not to be confused with the Princess Coronation ceremony, where Nataliya would receive an official royal tiara.

That would happen *after* the wedding.

Jenna's fashion magazine's photographer represented the favored press presence and would be the only press allowed to photograph the official coronation, while having access to areas the other media guests did not, as well.

Nikolai had made known his displeasure with news outlets that had run stories based on her father's spurious allegations of Nataliya's avarice and scheming. Excluding them from the official coronation was only part of it.

Which was why Jenna's photographer was in the room with Nataliya now as the stylist Jenna had recommended put the finishing touches on Nataliya's *look*.

"You definitely look regal enough to be The Princess of Mirrus, *Lady Nataliya*," Jenna teased, using the title she never did when they were alone.

Nataliya had been pleasantly surprised when no one suggested she choose someone with a higher rung on the social ladder than Jenna to be her maid of honor and said so now. "I'm so glad you're here with me. I'm pretty sure I'd be a bundle of nerves otherwise."

"I think the fact you are marrying the man of your dreams has more to do with why happiness is overriding nerves, but who am I to say?" Jenna responded with a laugh. "And there never was any chance someone might argue your choice to have me as your only attendant. Your mom and King Hotty put the kibosh on any dissent before you even floated my name to the wedding planner."

"How do you know that?" Nataliya demanded.

"Because unlike you, my dear friend, *I* listen to gossip."

Nataliya just laughed and got ready to promise the rest of her life to serving the people of Mirrus, as their King's Princess.

The Russian Orthodox church that hosted the wedding had been built the first decade of Mirrus' settlement.

The gorgeous structure had been the setting for every wedding in the House of Merikov since. Like Saint Basil's in Moscow, Mirrus' cathedral had multicolored rather than gold conical-topped spires, but inside the gold-leafed icons were lavish works of art from another century, and the intricately designed floor tiles breathtaking.

Her gown a replica of the one worn by the first and most beloved Queen of Mirrus in the country's history trailed behind Nataliya down the center aisle in thirty feet of rustling satin train. The guests filling the church were in a hazy glow, but Nikolai, waiting at the front for her, was in sharp focus.

He looked unutterably handsome in his Head of State military regalia, but even wearing an off-the-rack suit, she knew this man would leave her breathless.

The expression in his steely gray gaze when she joined him at the front of the church was so intense, it sent goose bumps along her arms and made her breath catch.

This man had a plan and she was part of it.

During the *procession* Nataliya was glad she had practiced negotiating her train or this moment could have been an unmitigated disaster. She was even more relieved that she would be changing into a more modern gown created by a high-end Russian designer before attempting to circulate at the reception later.

She wasn't thinking about her dress, or her need to stay very still not to mess up the train, when the priest began to speak the words of the age-old ceremony in Russian. He repeated each vow in Ukrainian before Nikolai and Nataliya made their promises.

Her heart pounding in her chest, Nataliya was surprised at how profound the moment felt.

She knew she loved the man she was marrying. Accepted that he did not love her, but she had not considered how bound to him the vows she spoke would make her feel.

She had anticipated the weight of her role as his Princess settling on her, but not this feeling that her heart and her life were irrevocably tied to this man. To a king.

The look in Nikolai's eyes said he felt a similar level of profundity.

Which perhaps should not have surprised her, but it did.

He kept his promises. Knew she kept hers.

It was a moment of total connection between them.

They were both making commitments they intended to keep. Absolutely.

As much as Nataliya was not a fan of big gatherings, she put on her game face, smiling until her cheeks ached as she was introduced or reacquainted with the upper echelon of society.

She accepted every good wish on her future happiness with a king with equal warmth, refusing to allow the hundredth thank you be any less sincere than the first.

However, when Jenna sidled up next to her and asked if she was ready to go, Nataliya wanted to shout, *Yes*!

She couldn't though. "We've got hours yet," she informed her best friend in an apologetic whisper.

"Not according to your husband, you don't."

Nataliya startled and looked around for Nikolai. "What do you mean?"

They'd spent more of the reception together than she had expected, but it would have been impossible to remain at one another's side throughout the evening.

And now, she couldn't see him anywhere.

"His Highness sent me to get you."

"Get me?" Nataliya felt like she wasn't tracking.

"He said something about a promise he made about your wedding night?" Jenna prompted.

Heat washed into Nataliya's cheeks. No way was she going to explain that particular promise to even her best friend.

"Where is he?" she asked.

Jenna nodded her head toward the south doors to the palace ballroom. "Come with me."

Somehow, Jenna, who had not been born to nobility, was negotiating the room like a seasoned campaigner. She had Nataliya in the corridor outside mere minutes later, explaining to anyone who impeded their progress that His Highness needed Princess Nataliya for something.

Unsurprisingly, a security detail waited, but neither of the men said anything as Jenna continued to lead the way to one of the hidden hallways used by the royal family to navigate the palace. Then they were going through a set of thick doors that led to the outside behind the palace where a sleek black limousine waited.

One of the security detail stepped forward to open the door and help Nataliya inside, still silent.

The interior of the limousine was empty but for her cell phone on the seat. She picked it up and settled onto the soft leather. It rang in her hand as she was reaching for the seat belt.

Nikolai's face flashed on the screen.

She answered. "Really? You changed my ringtone for your calls?"

"I thought it was appropriate." Amusement warmed his voice.

"Somehow I don't think of you when I think of modern hip-hop."

"And yet the song is very appropriate."

It was a modern ballad by a popular female artist about desire and fidelity. Not a song she would have thought he even knew. "Not exactly subtle." As all things royal should be.

In a hip-hop song. Who knew?

"You may want to change it later," he conceded.

And she smiled. He'd made the change as part of this special night.

"Where are you?" Should that have been her first question? Maybe.

"In the SUV in front of you."

She remembered there being an SUV in front of the limousine and one behind. A quiet cavalcade without the flags of station waving.

"Why there and not here?" she asked.

"You deserve a very special wedding night. Not for our first time together to be in the back of a limousine." The promise in his voice sent shivers of desire through her.

Nataliya's hand tightened on the phone. "And if you were here, it would be?" she goaded.

"Of a certainty."

How was it possible for the sexual intensity between them to be so hot? "Is it always like this?" she wondered aloud.

"No," he assured her in a growl. "It is not. What we have is uncommon."

But not love. Not on his side anyway. "Was it like this with your first wife?"

He inhaled, like the question shocked him, but he answered. "At first, something like it, but looking back I realize that it was never this intense. Maybe because Tiana and I didn't wait." He paused, like he was thinking. "I don't know, but as much as I desired her, there was never a time I thought I wouldn't be able to control myself if I was with her."

And he felt that way with Nataliya? She couldn't help liking that, but she didn't doubt that if *she* told him no, ever, he would control himself just fine. He meant he didn't think they could control themselves together.

"Like that first kiss in the garden." Neither of them had been showing any sort of control then.

"Yes."

"At first?" she asked. "Will it get less intense?"

"No," he said without hesitation.

"But you said that with Queen Tiana…" Nataliya allowed her voice to trail off.

He knew what she was talking about.

"What I had with my first wife was different," he said with certainty. "I was enthralled by her. She used sex to control, to manipulate, but I didn't realize it until we'd been married more than a year."

No question he was alone in the back of the SUV with the privacy window up. Just as she was. Or they would not be having such an intimate and revealing conversation.

Nataliya shifted, trying to alleviate the feeling of need that even talking about his dead wife was in no way diminishing. "Even if that's true, I cannot imagine she wasn't just as enthralled by you."

"Because you are." Nikolai sounded very satisfied by that fact.

"You know I am."

"We are well matched."

"Yes." She could not deny it. Nor could she deny that she wished he was with her, the setting of their first time sharing full intimacy be damned.

"Where are we going?"

"Somewhere we can have that spectacular wedding night you demanded."

"How long until we get there?"

"Only about forty-five minutes."

"Did you just say *only*?" she demanded.

"Relax, *kiska*, we will be there before you know it. I

will keep you entertained." And he did, telling her his plans for the night ahead.

By the time the limousine stopped, Nataliya was so hot and bothered she couldn't fumble her seat belt open. When she finally got it, she surged toward the door with no sense of aplomb and even less reticence.

Nikolai was there to take her hand. He practically yanked her from the car and right into his embrace.

"Lost your cool, Your Highness?" she asked him breathlessly as her body pressed against his hardness, her own cool nowhere in evidence.

"*Da*," he growled out, reverting to Russian. He told her he wanted her, that she was too beautiful to resist, in the same language. Then he swept her high against his chest.

She gulped in air and tried to regain a little of her equilibrium. "I thought carrying the bride over the threshold was a western tradition."

He didn't reply. Didn't look at her, just focused on covering the distance to the door of the mountain chalet in long, impatient strides.

Something in the corner of her vision caught her eye and Nataliya gasped. "You brought me to a glacier?"

The chalet sat high on a craggy hill overlooking a pristine blue glacier.

"Tomorrow," he gritted out as the door swung open in front to them.

"Tomorrow, what?"

"Talking." He acknowledged the woman who had opened to the door with a nod, but no words.

Nataliya gave the older woman a little wave and received a warm, very amused, smile in return.

Nataliya nuzzled into the curve of where his shoulder and neck met. "You're in kind of a hurry, huh?"

His big body gave a shudder, but he didn't slow down as he carried her determinedly up the stairs. And then they were in a huge master bedroom, the solid door slamming when he kicked it closed.

She would have teased him about slamming doors, but suddenly *that* moment was upon her. They were going to make love…have sex. Whatever they called it, Nataliya knew it would change her forever.

Her King made no move to let her go.

Inhaling his delicious masculine scent, she pressed a kiss to his neck, letting her tongue flick out to taste.

Everything inside her tightened, the pleasant throb between her legs she'd had for the last thirty minutes of the drive up the mountain becoming a sensual ache.

With a groan, Nikolai released her and then quickly stepped back, putting distance between them that she did not want.

She moved to follow him, but he put his hands up as if warding her off.

"What?" she demanded.

"You are a virgin."

"So? Tomorrow, I won't be."

"Precisely." He turned toward the door.

She stood in stunned silence until his hand landed on the handle. "Where are you going?" she demanded.

"You need gentle."

That was debatable. Nataliya wasn't feeling *gentle* right now. She was *hot and bothered*.

"So?"

"So, I need some time."

"Why?"

"So I can give you gentle."

"I don't want gentle," she informed him.

He spun to face her. "You think that, but—"

"Stop, right there," she interrupted. "Be very careful before you try to claim you know more about what I want and need than I do. I am a twenty-eight-year-old woman. I am a virgin by choice, not because the men in my life knew what was best for me and protected poor little old me."

And being a virgin did not mean she was ignorant about sex, or her own body's needs.

"You will be a passionate advocate for the rights of women in Mirrus."

"Right now, I'm not thinking of anyone but us." She stepped out of her shoes. "Either you respect me enough to let me make my own choices, or you don't."

She waited, wondering if she could have misjudged this man and his intentions so badly.

Air filled her lungs in a breath of relief as his hand dropped from the doorknob. "It is a matter of physical necessity, not believing I know your body better than you do."

It so was, but she could forgive him because he wasn't in possession of all the facts.

"I have toys," she told him baldly.

"What?" He stumbled back, like her words profoundly shocked him.

"I am a twenty-eight-year-old woman. If you have a fantasy of a naive virgin in your bed, we can play that scenario out sometime, but right now I just want *you*."

"What kind of toys?"

She rolled her eyes. "I'll show them to you some-time. Maybe you'll want to use them with me, but not tonight."

His already dark eyes flared with heated desire. "No. Not tonight."

Done with the waiting. Done with *any* delays, Nataliya reached behind her back and pulled the zip down on the designer dress she'd changed into for the reception.

He didn't ask what she was doing, or make any more sweet but inane comments about how she needed gentleness when Nataliya was so hot she thought she might combust if he didn't get inside her soon.

Nikolai stripped with more speed than finesse, baring his gorgeous body to Nataliya's eyes.

He was beyond fit. Muscles bulged on his biceps and chest, usually hidden by the formal attire of a king, his sculpted thighs showing why he'd found carrying her up the stairs so easy.

She let out a pent-up breath, her own dress a pool around her feet. "You are beautiful."

"I believe those are my words to you."

Her throat had gone dry and she couldn't reply with a witticism, just shook her head. He was everything she could have imagined wanting in an intimate partner.

She didn't need physical perfection, but it was standing right in front of her and she had no more words to tell him how turned on he made her.

The sight of his masculine body finished what his words on the phone had started and she *wanted*. She *needed*.

She went to shove her panties down her legs, but he was there just that quickly. His hands over hers. "Let me."

She nodded, her own hands sliding out from under his to press against his sculpted chest. She circled the eraser-hard nubs of his nipples, brushed her fingertips over them just as he undid the catch on her bra, releasing her breasts. Her already turgid nipples tightened as they were exposed to the air.

They both gasped.

He cupped her breasts, swiping his thumb over the hardened peaks. "You fit my hands too perfectly."

She moaned at the sensation coursing through her, but passivity was not on her agenda. Nataliya leaned forward and took one of his small male nipples delicately between her teeth, gratified by the groan of pleasure that came from her royal husband.

She'd read that some men loved having their nipples played with, some didn't like it, and some didn't care either way, but it did nothing for them. She was glad he was of the first type. She liked getting the kind of reaction she was getting from him.

His impressive erection jutted out insistently from his body, the head brushing against her skin and exciting her even more.

The years she'd fantasized about this man were nothing compared to the reality of having the freedom to touch as she pleased and the knowledge he wanted to do the same to her.

She kissed a trail upward until their mouths met again; all the while his hands were busy pulling sensual pleasure from her body with knowing touches to her breasts.

Without breaking the kiss, he pushed her panties down her thighs. He waited for her to step out of them and then dropped to his knees to brush her thigh-high stockings down with caresses along her inner thighs, then pulled them from her feet with sensual mastery.

This man understood a woman's body and how to give intense pleasure.

Nikolai shifted back just a little and then looked his fill at her now naked body. "*Krasiva.*"

"I thought that was my word for you," she said breathlessly, her knees threatening to buckle.

"You said it in English."

She would have laughed, but he ran a probing finger between the folds of her most intimate flesh. A strangled sound came out of Nataliya as she was touched so very intimately.

Nikolai surged back to his feet, pulling her into his body, rubbing against her with no evidence of reluctance. His hands cupped both her breasts and squeezed. The air in her lungs left her in a whoosh and though she gulped in air, Nataliya couldn't catch her breath.

Not with the way he touched her.

No hesitation, no excessive gentleness. He played with her breasts while she mapped his body with her hands.

She tilted her head and then they were kissing again, the hunger between them voracious and unabated. They kept kissing and touching until they fell together on the bed, their bodies pressed so tightly together she could feel every nuance of the ridge of his erection against her stomach.

He rolled them and she spread her legs, encouraging him to shift so his steel hardness rubbed against her clitoris.

She tilted up, seeking more stimulation, but it wasn't enough.

He reached down and pressed a finger inside her.

Pleasure rolled over her, her womb contracting in a moment of ecstasy unlike any she'd ever felt on her own. He pushed upward with his finger, hitting that spot inside so rich with nerve endings. Her climax crested again and she screamed, the sound swallowed by his mouth.

He caressed her through the ecstasy, but even though she'd just had the most intense orgasm of her life, her body was craving more.

And he gave it to her.

Nikolai pushed her thighs just a little wider and pressed inside, stretching swollen and slick flesh with his rigid erection.

"Yes!" she cried out, the sensation of him inside her absolutely perfect.

The pain of him pushing through her virginal barrier was masked by the incredible sensual pleasure racking her body. Clearly trusting her to know what she wanted, he set a hard and fast rhythm. She tilted her pelvis upward, matching his movements, demanding more with her body.

Their bodies grew slick with sweat, their breaths mingling in panted pleasure and the ecstasy built again.

"Come for me," he demanded as he pistoned into her body with unfettered passion.

"You come for me," she gasped back.

Everything inside her contracted in a rictus of pleasure so strong she could not even scream. His body went rigid and Nikolai tossed his head back, a primal shout coming from deep in his chest.

Every little move of his body triggered aftershocks of pleasure in hers. His groans said he was experiencing the same.

"That was amazing," she said with panting breaths.

He didn't reply with words, but kissed her, his lips soft and perfect against hers in the aftermath of such a primal loving.

She didn't know how long they remained connected like that.

But eventually Nikolai rolled off her, his arm going around her waist. "I suppose you want to take a shower."

"I do?" she asked, having no thought of doing so.

"We are all sweaty."

"So?" Sex was supposed to be messy, wasn't it?

"You don't mind?"

"Do you?" she asked, really not wanting to move, even for a shower.

"No." He nuzzled into her shoulder. "I love that you smell like both of us together."

"How primitive of you," she teased.

He went to shift away from her but she followed, leaning forward to kiss his muscular chest. "I like it too. Let's be throwbacks together."

The rigidity that had come over his body relaxed. "You do?"

"Hmm mmm." She snuggled into her new husband. "Thank you."

"For?" he asked, like he didn't want to misunderstand.

"Listening to me. For treating me like a woman and not just a princess."

"I will always try to listen to you."

Even his promises were perfect. He knew he couldn't promise to always get it right. Only to try.

"And I will always try to listen to you."

CHAPTER TWELVE

NIKOLAI AND NATALIYA lay together for a while, pressed together from chest to hip and Nataliya reveled in the intimacy of it.

But they had been on sexual edge for too long and the desire between them incvitably built again.

This time, he was gentle and teasing, showing her just how much pleasure he could bring to her body with a slow buildup. She returned his touches, learning what made him moan, what made him give that contented growl that said she was connecting to him more than sensually.

She wanted to be on top during their coupling this time and he let her without hesitation. Nataliya brought them both to another culmination of pleasure and collapsed onto him after.

Eventually, they did make it to the bath, where she learned the slide of naked bodies in the water could be terribly arousing.

The sun was rising over the glacier out the huge wall of windows when she and Nikolai finally settled into sleep, their bodies entwined.

They slept away the morning, but rose to have lunch

together. The entire side of the chalet facing the glacier seemed to be made of windows, so the dining room overlooked the incredible view just as the master bedroom did.

"This place is amazing."

"It is our personal getaway."

"You mean the family doesn't use it?" she asked in surprise before dishing some more fruit onto her plate.

She was ravenous.

"Not without my permission and with rare exception, I do not give it. The people of Mirrus can visit the glacier from the other side of the chasm."

"Aren't tourists allowed?"

"No. The park is owned by the royal family and only open to the people of Mirrus."

Conservation was a big thing on the island, so she wasn't surprised. "But the chalet is *yours*, not the royal family's?"

"Yes." He placed another fluffy pancake on her plate, seeming to enjoy watching her eat so enthusiastically. "It is a retreat for the King."

Nataliya looked around herself with satisfaction. "It's the perfect honeymoon destination." It afforded the privacy that would be lacking in their daily life and she was really happy to know they had this retreat to come to when they needed it.

"I'm so glad you think so."

Something about the way he said it gave Nataliya pause. "Didn't Queen Tiana like it?"

"She never came. Nature was not her thing."

"But it's so beautiful."

"Tiana had no interest in seeing the glacier. She refused to go anywhere she could not be entertained."

"You two weren't very well suited." Nataliya sucked in her breath and nearly bit her tongue in her chagrin saying something like that. "I'm sorry. It's not my place to judge your past relationship."

But he wasn't offended. Nikolai's smile was approving and warm. "If not you, then who?" He sipped his coffee. Black, no sugar or cream. So not how Nataliya enjoyed the bitter elixir. "You are right. Once we were married, I realized how little in common I had with my wife."

"That must have been hard, but still, you loved each other." And Nataliya was just realizing how very much she wanted that emotion from him.

"Love?" he mused. "I thought I did, but now I'm not so sure. She had me sexually enthralled. *She* was enthralled by the idea of being a queen."

"I'm sure she loved you." How could Queen Tiana have felt anything else for this amazing man?

"Are you? I am not." He didn't sound like he was bothered by that fact.

But she knew he had to be. She remembered how he'd been with Queen Tiana. Whatever he thought now, Nikolai had loved the other woman. And while that hurt Nataliya a little, she recognized that their marriage would probably be a much happier one.

Nikolai asked, remembered pain reflected in his steely gray eyes, "If she loved me, would she have gone skiing on that dangerous slope, knowing she was pregnant with my child?"

"She was very athletic," Nataliya offered. "Her sports acumen was renowned."

Queen Tiana had been known for her skiing prowess as well as her skydiving feats. She was very good at any sport she tried and she always did the most challenging aspect of those sports. The former Queen had been lucky right up until the end too, never having broken so much as a pinky in all her exploits.

"I'm sure Queen Tiana never even considered it might not go well for her to take that slope."

"I've never been sure. Yes, she enjoyed the adrenaline rush of high-risk sports, but she was a queen, pregnant with the heir to the throne." He looked at Nataliya with an expression she could not read. "Tiana did not want to be pregnant. She had wanted to wait to have children, but her birth control failed."

"All this time, I thought she didn't know," Nataliya admitted.

Everything in the media, every statement given by the palace, it had all said at the time that the tragedy was made worse by her taking a chance she hadn't realized she was taking.

"That she was pregnant? Oh, she knew. As I said, she wasn't happy about it. She refused to allow her pregnancy to curtail any of her pleasures."

Nataliya didn't know what to say. She couldn't imagine making the same choices as Queen Tiana, but those choices had been the other woman's to make. Even if they felt incredibly selfish to Nataliya.

"I could tell my brother absolutely no when he wanted to participate in extreme sports," Nikolai said, frustration lacing his tone. "He recognizes my role as his King. My dead wife? With her, I had no authority."

Nataliya got what Nikolai was saying. Konstantin

had given up any hopes of participating in extreme sports because of his role as his brother's heir. Queen Tiana had disregarded not only her role as Queen, but the risk to her unborn child who would become the heir to the throne.

Even so. "Um… I don't really want you bossing me around like my sovereign either."

"What about as your husband? Do I have any sway over your actions in that regard?"

"Of course you do, just I expect you to listen to my counsel when something is important to me in regard to your actions. But ultimately, though we will listen to each other, we are still self-governing."

"You live in a monarchy now, you do realize this?"

"Yes. But you aren't the type of monarch to dictate the actions of your people."

"You think not?"

"I wouldn't have married you otherwise."

"Then I hope you will not be too disappointed to realize that I will not allow you to take the kind of risks Tiana did. Not with your own safety and definitely not with the safety of any of our future unborn children."

"You sound really stern right now."

"You do not sound intimidated, but I promise you. I learned my lesson."

"And I promise *you* that while I intend to make my own decisions, you never have to worry about me putting my own safety at risk or that of our children, born, or otherwise."

The only high risk she'd taken was the one to her heart by marrying him.

* * *

They went hiking that afternoon, the lush forest awash with summer plants and flowers. They didn't see as much wildlife as they might have done but for the security detail ahead of them and the one that came behind.

Too many people. Too much noise.

Nataliya didn't mind because nothing could detract from the beauty of Mirrus. And as much as she might enjoy seeing moose or even a wildcat, she wasn't keen to see a bear. Even a small brown one.

"I'm glad you haven't encouraged tourism to the detriment of this beauty," she told Nikolai as they walked.

"We have been fortunate that Mirrus Global and the other industries on the island have never been reliant on the tourist season."

"I know about the mining." Which posed its own challenges for conservation. "And the high-tech arm of Mirrus Global."

"Mirrus Global isn't the only high-tech company we have based here. One of the world's most advanced AI developers is a citizen and his company employs many others."

"I'd like to meet him."

"Of course you would." Nikolai smiled down at her with indulgence.

Since the barely banked desire was there as well, Nataliya didn't take offense.

"Nevertheless, a certain amount of tourism is beneficial." He took her hand and kissed the back as if unaware of doing so. "If for no other reason, than offering an opportunity for our people to meet potential partners from a new gene pool."

She laughed, thinking he was joking but realized he wasn't "You're serious. That happens? A lot?"

"Enough to make the management of our tourism industry worth the headache it brings to environmental and resource management."

"Although the education system through high school is top-notch on Volyarus, Uncle Fedir has fought against building a university every time the issue comes up. Maybe that's why." She'd spent so many years living in the greater Seattle area that some of these nuances to a small, island country were new to her, despite having been born in Volyarus and being a member of its royal family.

Nikolai nodded. "We do not have a university for the same reason."

"But aren't you afraid young people won't return to the island?" she asked, thinking that had to be a real detriment.

But Nikolai shook his head. "We are both small countries, only able to support a finite population. Attrition is not always a bad thing. Voluntary attrition is preferred over involuntary."

Like her and her mother's exile?

But thinking about it, Nikolai's attitude about natural attrition made sense. If everyone stayed, both small countries would be very different places. They would be crowded. And the problems that came with higher populations would plague them. Higher crime. Unemployment. Poverty, etc.

"I never even considered that. Both countries have a lot of citizens working in other countries while maintaining their citizenship."

"Yes. And sometimes their children return to live."

"Do you allow immigration?"

"Our numbers are by necessity extremely low, but we have few requests for permanent residence. Living in a country that lacks the amenities of big cities because we do not have them and has months in the winter with only a few hours of sunlight isn't for everyone."

She considered that. "It is very isolated, but it's so beautiful."

"I am glad you think so. It is my hope you will find life here as fulfilling as I do."

They continued to hold hands as they walked, and Nataliya made no effort to overcome the illusion of intimacy and romance the small physical connection provided.

Their honeymoon lasted only a week, but Nikolai was a reigning monarch with duties even his father and brother could not perform in his place. And yet, during their honeymoon, he never once allowed state business to take precedence over their time together.

It was a heady feeling for Nataliya to be the center of her royal husband's attention.

And the sex?

Was off the charts. She learned he had no compunction about dragging her off to bed in the middle of the day. He learned that she was no retiring maiden, unwilling to initiate lovemaking.

They made love often and by the end of the week, Nataliya felt more connected to Nikolai than she ever had to another person.

* * *

Their first official state event as a married couple was the night after their return to the palace.

Nataliya did her best to maintain a cordial demeanor, but she spent most of the evening managing her response to subtle and even some overt bids to get her to speak to her husband on one matter or another.

She complained to Nikolai later as they were going to bed. "I don't understand what they hope to gain having me bring a topic up to you rather than them." Nataliya let the disgust she felt by the grasping behavior show in her tone.

"Perhaps they believe you will attempt to use my obvious affection for you to sway my opinion."

"Is your affection for me obvious?" She hadn't noticed him being all that affectionate since returning from their honeymoon.

In fact, his very dignified manner was taking some getting used to after such an intensely sensual week where they touched constantly, whether they were having sex, or not. He had been more overtly affectionate with her *before* their wedding than since their return to the palace.

Nataliya wished she knew what caused the difference. Because she'd look for a way to change it.

He looked chagrined whether by her question or his own thoughts, she couldn't tell.

"We have been home for thirty-six hours," he informed her like she didn't know. "In that time, I have texted you several times, eaten every meal in your company and called you for no other apparent reason than to check on your welfare."

"Um…you kept track?" She hadn't. Maybe she should have. Apparently that kind of communication indicated a *deep* affection on his part. Who knew?

His gorgeous lips twisted in grimace. "My aides have. And you can be sure that the gossip of my *besotted* state has spread like wildfire through the palace."

She crossed the huge bedroom they shared until she stood only a few inches away from him, but for some reason couldn't make herself reach out and touch him.

Perhaps them sharing a room was another indication of his regard? She knew her aunt and uncle did not, but she'd never considered their marriage all that healthy. At least not since becoming an adult and realizing her uncle had a "secret" lover.

"Did you share a room with Queen Tiana?" she asked out of curiosity.

"Naturally. This is not the nineteenth century."

She smiled. "No, it isn't. So, what do the gossips say about the *deep affection* I hold for you?"

He stilled, his hands on his unbuttoned shirt, his head swiveling so their gazes caught. "You hold me in *deep* affection?"

"Yes." It wasn't as if Nikolai didn't already know she had had feelings for him for a long time. She wasn't using the L word, might never use it, but he had to know her feelings ran deeply. "Didn't your aides point out my behavior?"

After all, she'd texted him just as often, answering any communication from him immediately, regardless what else she might be doing.

"No. They did not remark on it."

And it clicked. "They're worried about you."

"I believe so, yes." He went back to removing his clothes, his body shifting so he was turned more away from her than toward her.

"They know Queen Tiana influenced your decisions." And that must lacerate pride as deeply rooted as the King's.

He jerked his head in acknowledgment and then looked away, pushing his slacks down his thighs.

Refusing to be sidetracked by the sexy vision before her, Nataliya reached out and laid her hand on his arm. "You know I won't ever do that."

"I do." But he still wasn't looking at her.

"They don't."

"No."

"That is their problem," she pronounced.

He jerked back around to face her. "No, it is also my problem."

"No, it is not. You know I won't try to manipulate you. That's all that matters. Eventually, they will see that I'm not like her, but it is not on you to convince them."

"They have a right to be worried." And he hated admitting that.

That much was obvious.

"Sure," she acknowledged. "Just as my mom is going to worry about how you treat me until she sees for herself you aren't going to change into a monster."

His brows furrowed, offense coming over his features. "I promised you."

"You don't think my father ever promised never to hit her again, never to hurt me again?"

"I am not him." This time his tone left no doubt he was offended. Deeply.

"No, you are nothing like him," Nataliya agreed. "You are everything I could have ever hoped for in a husband."

"Unlike my brother."

"Even if your brother was as wonderful as you are, he has the singular disadvantage of not being you. It wasn't fair of me to sign that contract when I knew I cared for you."

"You were a child."

"I was legally an adult and the feelings I had for you were very adult." Nataliya no longer felt guilty for those feelings.

She knew the difference between having feelings and acting on them. She never had because he had been married and then she had been promised to his brother.

But now? She could do as she liked.

"You are my wife. You get to act on those adult feelings," he said, as if reading her mind.

The kiss they shared was incendiary and the love-making after had an emotional quality Nataliya couldn't define. And really? She was too tired and sated to even try.

She just snuggled into her husband's muscular body feeling safe and held in very deep affection.

A couple of weeks later, Nataliya was in the study in their suite, looking for some research she needed for a meeting she was supposed to attend with the labor council.

She had some ideas for employment-driven voluntary expatriate living she hoped they would be willing to listen to, but she was prepared for skepticism. Because so far, that was all she'd met with when she attended meetings in her official capacity as The Princess of Mirrus and a member of Nikolai's cabinet.

She'd been shocked when he'd given her an official title and list of duties that showed he regarded her as equal to his brothers and father. Even so, his cabinet ministers, business associates and other politicos treated her ideas with indulgence rather than attention.

Her mother reminded Nataliya that she had to build relationships before she would get the trust and sometimes even the respect Nataliya knew she would need to do her job as The Princess of Mirrus effectively.

It had not gone unnoticed that Nikolai made no indication he would be bestowing the title of Queen on her as he had his first wife.

Some took that to mean he had married Nataliya for mainly breeding purposes. She found such assumptions offensive. Yes, she would be giving birth to the heir to the throne, but that didn't make her a brood mare.

She didn't need to be Queen to hold an opinion or have a brain and use it.

Not that her job as The Princess of Mirrus was something she'd ever aspired to, but she would do it to the best of her abilities. It was how she was made. How her mother had raised her to be.

Nataliya could admit to herself, if no one else, that she enjoyed her couple of hours each day on the computer working in the elite tech department of Mirrus Global more than all the luncheons and meetings where she was treated like a nominal figure.

But she couldn't make changes if she didn't stay the course. And she'd noticed some changes that needed to be made.

For instance, as forward thinking as she considered Nikolai, she had done some deep digging and discovered a discrepancy in pay to female and male staff in senior positions both in the Mirrus Global and the palace staffs. She planned to address those with him in their meeting the following day.

She grabbed her papers and knocked a folder to the floor. Nataliya picked it up and recognized the logo for Yurkovich-Tanner.

Feeling no compunction about reading it, she flipped the folder open and started thumbing through the pages. It was a joint business proposal for the high-tech divisions of Mirrus Global and Yurkovich-Tanner, written by her cousin Demyan. So, it had been created with serious intention.

Demyan didn't put his name on anything he didn't believe in fully.

She would ask her husband what he thought of the proposal at their meeting the next day, as well.

Nikolai's administrative assistant showed Nataliya and her own personal assistant into the King's spacious office.

Nikolai stood on her entrance and indicated a set of sofas and chairs on the far side of the office. "Let's sit over here."

The dark paneling and nineteenth-century-style furniture gave off a decidedly royal vibe, but the hints at high-level technology were there to see if you recognized them.

Now that she was The Princess of Mirrus, Nataliya had an entire staff and her own set of offices, but all meetings with her husband were held in his.

Protocol.

It would be daunting if she hadn't been prepared for the changes coming into her life. At least that's what she told herself.

Nikolai took a seat kitty-corner to her, but far enough away to maintain professional distance. Again...protocol.

Someone came in with a coffee tray, but Nataliya didn't need more caffeine, so she ignored it. So did Nikolai.

He pulled out his tablet, looked down for a minute and then back up at her. "I've looked over the report you sent over. I agree we need to hire an equity auditor."

That had been easier than she expected, but she didn't make the mistake of saying so in front of their staff. She'd thought they'd have to take the report to the appropriate HR people. It was good to be King.

She smiled. "Thank you. Would you like me to take care of that, or did you have someone else in mind?"

"My staff will contact the firms you suggest in the addendum to your report."

She nodded. "That's wonderful." She was careful to monitor her enthusiasm, but Nataliya was thrilled and tried to let him know with her eyes.

His own eyes crinkled at the corners in a smile that did not reach his mouth. "We cannot allow such wage inequalities to continue."

"I agree."

They talked over some other things and he asked her opinion on taking Mirrus Global into a certain technology area. Offering her opinion also gave the opportunity to segue into asking what he was going to do about the combined venture proposal she had seen the day before.

"How did you know about that?" he asked, sounding wary.

She tilted her head, studying him and wondering where the wariness was coming from. "You left the prospectus on the desk in our study."

"I see." Rather than looking upset she had read it as she might have expected from his cautious reaction, tension leached from Nikolai's stance and expression. "And you thought, what?"

"On the face of it, it seems to be a win-win for both Mirrus Global and Yurkovich-Tanner, not to mention the two countries."

"Provided you trust Yurkovich-Tanner in their dealings with some of our most proprietary software."

"Well, yes." She frowned. "Don't you?"

"I make it a policy never to trust anyone outside my inner circle that completely."

That was not surprising. She'd be a lot more shocked if he was any other way. "That is understandable, but if you look at their track record, Demyan's office has never been responsible for a data leak." She smiled. "And he is your family now."

"Family are not always trustworthy," Nikolai said repressively.

Like Nataliya needed that reminder. "I am aware."

He nodded. "Good."

Not thrilled by his apparent lack of sensitivity where her dealings with her father were concerned, Nataliya nevertheless was ready to tackle the subject. "You said you had an update on the situation with the Count."

Nikolai jolted, like he was surprised by something. But she could not imagine what. Surely he expected her to ask?

After speaking with her mother, Nataliya had decided to press criminal charges against her father as well as filing a civil lawsuit against him.

"The first update is that he is no longer a count. While he has maintained his citizenship in Volyarus, he is no longer recognized as a member of its nobility and his exile has been formally extended to lifetime status."

"My uncle did all that?"

"You are calling him uncle again."

After a quick look at the staff and the security in the room, Nataliya nodded. "I have realized that life, not to mention our personal motivations, is complicated."

Nikolai inclined his head.

But Nataliya wasn't going to get any more private with her thoughts in front of an audience. "Is that all?"

"No. Danilo has been arrested and charged with attempted blackmail. He will be tried in Washington State. Both Mirrus and Volyarus have levied charges against him for crimes against the monarchy."

Chills ran down Nataliya's spine. "You insisted on that, didn't you?"

"Yes."

"Thank you." Her father would not be allowed to

hurt her mother again and that was the most important thing to Nataliya. "I'm surprised my uncle went along."

"I am not. He had more to lose refusing than to risk by doing what he should have so many years ago."

"Do you think the civil suit is still necessary?" she asked, thinking pretty strict measures had already been taken.

But Nikolai nodded. "The charges against him do not carry a life sentence. Although he will never be allowed on either Mirrusian or Volyarussian soil again unless he wants to face a trial for those charges, he could still do you and your mother damage from America."

"And you think a civil suit will prevent that?"

"Winning a civil suit against him will go a long way in preventing him filing charges against either of you."

"For what?"

"You need to ask? Danilo will manufacture whatever tale he needs to in order to pursue his own ends."

Nataliya frowned and nodded. It was nothing less than the truth. "You're right."

Nikolai smiled a politician's smile, not a lover's and asked, "Did you want to discuss anything else?"

"No, but I would like to make sure we have time to walk in the garden tonight."

He looked startled.

"I miss you," she admitted baldly.

Also, she *liked* him texting her throughout the day and calling her when he had the chance. She didn't want that to stop because his staff thought she was less invested than he was in their time together.

"I will make sure my schedule permits."

* * *

Though she was tired, their walk in the garden was everything Nataliya needed it to be.

Nikolai held her hand and reverted to the more openly affectionate man she found so hard to resist.

Not that she needed to resist him.

He might not trust her cousin implicitly, but Nataliya trusted Nikolai. She loved him. So much.

Her unusual exhaustion was explained later when she realized she'd started her monthly.

Her first couple of days always left her nearly comatose with tiredness. She took vitamins to combat the symptoms, but the supplements only helped so much.

She was practically falling asleep as she slid into bed late that evening. There had been another State dinner and they'd come up to their suite later than they usually did.

He reached for her and she snuggled into his body, but when he started to touch her intimately, she stayed his hand with her own. "Not tonight."

His reaction was electric. He sat up and the light went on. "So, this is it? This is how you react to me telling you no about something that benefits your family?"

"What are you talking about?" she asked, even his uncharacteristic response unable to wash the tiredness from her brain. "I just want to sleep."

"Last night, you did not want to sleep."

"Last night I wasn't having my period," she informed him with more honesty than finesse.

"You're having your monthly?" he asked, like the idea was a foreign concept.

"Yes. Sorry, no royal babies just yet."

He waved his hand like that wasn't important when in fact it was incredibly important. Especially to everyone else. Even her mom wanted to know if Nataliya was pregnant yet.

She'd only been married three weeks!

"I thought…"

"What did you think?" she asked, not sure she even wanted an answer.

"That you were angry I said no to Demyan's proposal."

"Did you say no to it?" She didn't remember Nikolai saying that.

"Well, not yet, but my plans are to turn it down."

"Okay."

"Okay?"

"Only I'm really tired. Can you hold me and let me sleep?" she spelled out for him.

He settled back down beside her, pulling her upper body onto his chest, his arms wrapped securely around her.

She went boneless against him, making a soft sound of approval.

"You don't care about the joint venture?" he asked into the darkened bedroom, something strange in his tone.

"Not enough to talk about it now. Can we talk in the morning?"

He kissed the top of her head. "Yes."

Nataliya woke with a sense that something wasn't right.

Nikolai's arms were still around her, though they

were spooning now. Which was definitely *right*. It was the light coming in through the windows.

"What time is it?" She tried to move his arm so she could get up. "We overslept!"

How was that possible? Nikolai *never* overslept and frankly, neither did she.

His hold on her tightened. She wasn't going anywhere. "Do not stress yourself. I arranged for our morning meetings to be moved."

"How?" Both their schedules were set in stone as far as the staff was concerned. "When?"

"How? I called my administrative assistant and had her call *your* personal assistant and social secretary. When? Last night after you fell asleep. I don't think a foghorn would have woken you, much less my voice talking on the phone."

"I was pretty tired." She felt a lot better that morning, her supplements and the extra sleep having done wonders. "It's always like that the first couple of days of my period. I'm sorry."

He grunted. It was not a kingly sound. At all.

But it carried a wealth of masculine meaning. "*You* have nothing to apologize for."

"But you do?" she asked as she turned in the band of his arms to face him.

His gorgeous cheekbones were scored with color. "I do."

"What?"

"I doubted you."

"What did you doubt?" She did her best to remember the night before and tried to figure out what he was talking about. He'd been weird all right, but she'd been too tired to worry on it then.

"Last night when you turned me down, I thought you were withholding sex to get your way." He looked and sounded as embarrassed as a king could be.

Good. He should be.

Withhold sex? From him? Chance would be a fine thing!

"My way about what?" she asked in confusion.

"The business venture with your cousin."

"I have a *way* about that?" she asked, still not sure she got where the disconnect was coming from.

"I thought you wanted me to say yes and were making sure I did so."

Nataliya sat up, giving him a look so he would loosen his arms. "We talked about that. I promised I would never do it. You said you believed me."

"I did believe you. I do believe you."

"Then what was last night about?" The things he'd said made a lot more sense now.

"It was about bad memories."

Nataliya got that. She really did. "I am not her."

It was his turn to sit up. They faced each other in the big bed. "No, you are not. You could hurt me so much more than Tiana ever did."

"What are you saying?" How could that be possible?

He was implying Nataliya had some emotional hold on him.

"I have come to realize that while I was sexually besotted with Tiana, I never really loved her. My grief on her death had more to do with what could have been than anything that was."

"Okay."

"I realized on our honeymoon that *I do love you* and knowing the depth of my feelings for you when you do not feel the same has made me…" He paused, took a deep breath and then offered. "Insecure."

"You love me?" she asked, the shock of such a possibility making her heart race and her face go all hot.

"With everything in me. My staff and cabinet are right to worry. I would move heaven and earth for you."

"But Nikolai, I do love you. I have since I was a teenager."

"That was not love. You felt attracted to me like I was attracted to Tiana. Love is a much deeper emotion."

"Do you remember what we learned on our wedding night?" she asked.

"That we are insanely sexually compatible?"

"That I know myself better than you do. After all, I am living in my skin."

"Yes, of course."

"So, when I say I love you, I mean it."

"You mean it?" The smile that came over his features was so vibrant it almost hurt to see. "You mean it! You love me."

"I do."

The intimacy that followed was shocking. She didn't know they could have sex this time of month, but showers were an amazing thing.

Later, they shared a leisurely breakfast on the balcony to their palace suite.

"Did you love me when you accepted my proposal?" he asked.

She refrained from rolling her eyes. Barely. He'd

been asking questions like this since they sat down.
"Yes."

"Did you *know* you loved me?"

"Yes."

"And when you made your vows…"

"I meant every one. Nikolai, I love you."

"Enough to forgive me for doubting you?"

"I was never actually angry."

"But—"

"Nikolai, we both brought damage into this marriage."

"Your damage doesn't have you accusing me of things I would never do."

She was glad he recognized she would never use him the way Tiana had. "My damage made it impossible for me to admit my love before you acknowledged yours."

And that shamed her. They'd both suffered pain because of her inability to offer emotional honesty.

"I did not tell you right away either."

"You realized you loved me on our honeymoon. Your timing has mine beat by a mile."

He grinned. "I do not care. You love me. That is all that matters to me."

"I've loved you half my life, it feels like. It's a permanent condition."

"Nothing could make me happier."

He named her Queen of Mirrus on their first anniversary and she wore a dress and robes that had to be accommodated for her tiny baby bump. They made it into the media spotlight often because the love between the King and Queen of Mirrus had the world enthralled.

It was the romance of the century.

Nataliya never cared about stuff like that, but waking every morning with the knowledge she was loved so completely made each day better. Her very dignified husband showed an affectionate side no one thought he had.

A side he had never shown another.

Nataliya was honored to be his Queen, but she adored being his wife.

And Nikolai made it clear every single day, in small and big ways that he adored being her husband.

* * * * *

Adored Queen by Royal Appointment?
Look out for the next installment in
the Princesses by Royal Decree trilogy!

Why not also explore these other
Lucy Monroe stories?

An Heiress for His Empire
A Virgin for His Prize
Kostas's Convenient Bride
The Spaniard's Pleasurable Vengeance
After the Billionaire's Wedding Vows...

Available now!

WE HOPE YOU ENJOYED
THIS BOOK FROM
HARLEQUIN
PRESENTS

Escape to exotic locations where passion knows no bounds.

Welcome to the glamorous lives of royals and billionaires, where passion knows no bounds. Be swept into a world of luxury, wealth and exotic locations.

8 NEW BOOKS AVAILABLE EVERY MONTH!

HPHALO2021

#3925 THE BILLION-DOLLAR BRIDE HUNT
by Melanie Milburne

Matteo has an unusual request for matchmaker Emmaline: he needs a wife who *isn't* looking for love! But the heat burning between them at his Italian villa makes him wonder if *she's* the bride he wants.

#3926 ONE WILD NIGHT WITH HER ENEMY
Hot Summer Nights with a Billionaire
by Heidi Rice

Executive assistant Cassie has orders to spy on tech tycoon Luke. While he's ultra-arrogant, he's also aggravatingly irresistible. Before Cassie knows it, they're jetting off to his private island—and her first-ever night of passion!

#3927 MY FORBIDDEN ROYAL FLING
by Clare Connelly

As crown princess, I must protect my country...*especially* from infuriatingly sexy tycoons like Santiago del Almodovár! He wants to build his disreputable casino on my land. And I want to deny our dangerous attraction!

#3928 INVITATION FROM THE VENETIAN BILLIONAIRE
Lost Sons of Argentina
by Lucy King

To persuade the formidable Rico Rossi to reunite with his long-lost brother, PR expert Carla Blake must accept his invitation to Venice. She knows not to let powerful men get too close, but can she ignore their all-consuming attraction?

HPCNMRB0621

Get 4 FREE REWARDS!

We'll send you 2 FREE Books plus 2 FREE Mystery Gifts.

Harlequin Presents books feature the glamorous lives of royals and billionaires in a world of exotic locations, where passion knows no bounds.

FREE
Value Over
$20